THE BOARDERS IN THE RUE MADAME

The
Boarders
in the
Rue Madame

Nine Gallic Tales

by HALLIE BURNETT

William Morrow & Company, Inc.
New York   1966

Copyright © 1960, 1961, 1962, 1966 by Hallie Burnett

Three of the stories in this book
have been published in *Story*.

Published simultaneously in Canada by
George J. McLeod Limited, Toronto.

Printed in the United States of America.

Library of Congress Catalog Card Number 66-24964

Contents

Oh, you may be sure that this drama is no work of fiction, no mere novel! It is all true, so true, that everyone may recognize its elements within himself, perhaps in his very heart.

—HONORÉ DE BALZAC, *Père Goriot*

Lady from the
Cape of Good Hope

The moment Ruby Fairlie took her place at the Pension du Coeur table, Amanda Cook looked at her husband as apprehensively as the other wives were looking at theirs. It was not that Ruby Fairlie could be classed as pretty, being shapely and bold rather than petite and mignonne, but there was no doubt she looked like a silent motion picture version of a *femme fatale*. Her full red lips curved with sensuous richness, her coiffure was sleek as brown sealskin, and her firm flesh had a glow such as healthy and frequently petted babies have. Her movements were slow, without waste, and indicated a mysterious quality of attraction which made mere prettiness seem unimportant.

"Mrs. Fairlie comes to Paris from South Africa," Mademoiselle du Coeur informed them that first day.

"South Africa—hmmm," murmured Professor Henry Cook, who was not usually susceptible but who now stared at this bright hibiscus of a woman as though he were at that moment touring her native land. And the handsome blond head of George Cramer, at the moment the pension's only

American bachelor, was alerted from his glass of vin ordinaire.

"Naturally, I'm a British subject," Mrs. Fairlie said, with an odd twist of her pectoral muscles which they discovered, in time, to be an assertion of dignity but which now appeared as arch coquetry. "Some foreigners don't seem to understand that."

They were used to being called "foreigner" in Paris, so not even the sophisticated Mr. Cramer took offense, although he reflected that the designation was not one generally used by a South African wench who was a "foreigner" herself. He had only half a mind on what she was saying, however, the other half being on the curious rhythm of her body—fascinating indeed to one of George Cramer's rather specialized experience.

Mrs. Cook, observing this motion, had a brief hope that the woman was Negro, but such comfort died when she observed that Mrs. Fairlie's nose was white-skinned and delicately retroussé, her violet eyes imperceptibly slanted upward, and her rather small, soft hands were whiter than Mrs. Cook's own.

"I myself have visited Capetown, Johannesburg and Pretoria," Professor Cook informed Mrs. Fairlie encouragingly. "Delightful society there in my, ah, salad days," he asserted.

"Capetown's not bad," she admitted carelessly, turning with more concentrated interest to her *tomates provençal*. "You can have the rest."

Meanwhile the younger women were noticing Mrs. Fairlie's close fitting marine-blue jacket and speculating whether the diamond horseshoe pin on her left lapel was real. If she was that rich, why would she be stopping at this Left Bank pension, which was all most of them here could afford? And why had she come North on a freighter as she, this moment, was telling Mlle du Coeur?

"Of course the Captain was a great friend of mine," Mrs. Fairlie confided, as thought she had read their thoughts, and the young women hastily veiled their eyes. "A charming gentleman—You've no idea," she finished vaguely, but her smile suggested a satisfaction more explicit.

George Cramer stared a moment, then ran a big hand over his mat of golden hair and down over his mouth as he murmured to Mrs. Cook, mischievously, at his side. "And the Captain must have found our Mrs. Fairlie a 'charming' lady, too, I've no doubt!"

Amanda Cook giggled and felt better, for at least the lady from the Cape of Good Hope had failed to impress George Cramer, even if Professor Cook was still staring at her with undiminishing delight.

Ruby was not pleased as she regarded the guests around the pension table. Even if she had no better place to go at the moment, and one nook was as good as another while deciding whether to divorce her husband or return to him, naturally she'd hoped for a little diversion while making up her mind. This place was as sexless as the boarding school she'd run away from at sixteen to marry Cyril!

Fortunately, Ruby had a healthy appetite for many delicacies, and the food of the Pension du Coeur was excellent. As she consumed the first course rapidly and with pleasure, she reflected how Cyril had so often spoiled things by pointing out that hasty indulgence of the appetite was in bad taste: he and his sister ate and drank always as though taking Holy Communion—although in the early days he himself had been greedy enough in bed. Now Ruby helped herself generously to two large and succulent portions of roast veal from the platter held at her left elbow and thought, thank God, neither of them is around to see me now!

"Ah, non, non, Madame! Un morceau. Un seul!" cried
the bonne, while a skinny adolescent at one end of the
table choked with laughter.

"Et pourquoi un seul?" Ruby demanded. Then, as her
violet eyes raced the length of the table she saw, unbeliev-
ably, one small portion of meat in the center of each plate.
With such irritability that the platter tipped like an over-
loaded boat, and a drop of brown gravy splashed on the
pink Aubusson carpet, she put one morsel back and looked
sulkily at Mlle du Coeur.

Then, unfortunately, George Cramer showed his first
weakness. An affable man whom women pursued without
much success, he certainly should have known better than
to waste sympathy on Mrs. Fairlie. Yet now he leaned forward in his disarmingly boyish way to console her. "We've
all had our knuckles cracked for that at least once, Mrs.
Fairlie," he said sympathetically.

To be sure, he turned immediately afterward to Mademoiselle with the tact for which he was famous. "Mam'selle,
you keep us much too well-fed," he said, leaning back in his
chair to emphasize the fine, contented state of his body. But
it was too late. Ruby Fairlie was already appraising him
with frank and obvious pleasure and now thrust up her
pretty white hands in a gesture of apology and remorse.

"I must have looked an awful piggy," she admitted, happily. "But never again," she promised in very good French,
"will I commit such an error at your table, Mam'selle."

Mademoiselle's eyes flickered over the spot of gravy on her
carpet and she bowed coldly; and as the meal went on and
Ruby heaped four lavish spoonsful of sugar on her *petit-
suisse*, the Frenchwoman seemed even less inclined to speak
in pleasantries.

Ruby would have left that first day if Mr. Cramer had

not come to life. She was a woman who set great store by "nice" things, and she had not been pleased with the service, the heavy glass water pitchers, or the thick bottles of vin ordinaire on the coarse white cloth. Could anyone imagine, in good Colonial society, putting a glass block beside a plate to carry over a knife and fork from one course to the next?

Before Captain Jimmy left for Capetown with his ship he had found her a first-class hotel off the Champs Élysées, but she hadn't felt safe with all those Frenchmen ogling her in the lobby. Besides, francs had a way of simply flying out of one's pocket in an arrondissement where every café and shop was so seductive, and she had got to feeling Fate was using her unbearably when this pension was recommended by that good-looking young man at the American Express—she had thought he might look her up once she moved in.

After a few days sitting opposite George Cramer she forgot about the young man, however, and the Captain, too— even with four wonderful weeks at sea a good bouncy woman couldn't live forever on what she'd had—but she admitted that the American was a puzzler. Blowing hot, then cold, staring at her one moment so it made her very skin quiver, and the next gazing over her head as if she were not there, he looked enough like Captain Jimmy for her to be sure he would act in a hurry once he made up his mind. With that broad, bold chin, that arrogant nose and voice like a bishop's, and the quick, athletic drive of his body, he was certainly a man to consider. While from the click of preparedness in her heart, like a camera loaded and set for action (which had signalled her readiness for love during most of the thirty-eight years of her life), she knew it was but a matter of time before she found herself in his bed, or he in hers.

George Cramer, no less conscious of Ruby than she of him—although perhaps in a different way—stared at the woman's white rounded forehead and milk-smooth cheeks, reflecting how the planes of some women's faces were as female as their breasts, and was scared half to death. Yet he was too intrigued now to turn away, even though to delay might cost a man in his committed bachelor state more than George was prepared to give.

There had not been a romance at the pension for some time, and even Mademoiselle, a most circumspect woman, was interested in this one. True, her favorite expression was: "There has never been any immorality in the Pension du Coeur." And within Ruby's hearing she had added, "Mama would not permit this!"

"But 'Mama' is bedridden," murmured Ruby in an aside to her neighbor, Professor Cook. At the moment Mama's illness was unhappily a fact.

"True, but I am not," said the daughter, firmly, and Ruby had the grace to flush.

Yet from the beginning Mademoiselle kept George Cramer and the lady from South Africa seated face to face, thus insuring such lively conversation between the two that guests at the other table strained to hear what was going on. Mr. Cramer had always been amusing, but after Ruby Fairlie arrived he created conversational extravagances which aroused in Mrs. Fairlie an inexhaustible appreciation that animated George Cramer like the voices of a multitude.

Yet it all seemed to end there, for apparently no meeting between the two took place in the cafés of Paris or in any more private place. Mrs. Cook and the Professor, on the same floor as Mr. Cramer, knew he kept no later hours than before, and had no visitors in his room; and anyone could see how conversation between the two was picked up from one meal to the next. It was perhaps natural after a while for Ruby Fairlie to look at George a bit sharply, as though she'd

been waiting for him somewhere and he had failed to come.
. . . There was no doubt about it, her presence did create di-
versions for the pension.

As, for instance, the time when she said to Professor
Cook, whose dignity still awed even his little wife, "Where
did you pick up that fine French accent, Professor? You
must have had a jolly good sleeping companion to be that
good."

This had sent them into stifled laughter, the Professor
being the kind of man he was. And if the laughter of
George Cramer seemed less spontaneous than the others',
at least he stared at Ruby as though never before had he seen
her equal.

Another time Julian, the long-legged American adolescent, asked, "You ever find any diamonds down there in
South Africa, Mrs. Fairlie?"

Mrs. Fairlie shrugged and pouted. "The blooming old
government hoards them," she said. "You couldn't keep one
if you did find it! But once when I was a little girl my
brother and I kicked a rock and found—"

Talking reminiscently about the diamond she had found,
she could hardly have been prepared for the sudden attention of the entire table, which she was able to hold for five
minutes without exerting an ounce of sex appeal. Even
George Cramer got her to talk on and on like a boy whose
dreams of adventure perhaps held images as youthful as
Julian's, as well as the more mature ones natural to a man
his age.

Ruby, however, was becoming restless. A born boudoir
actress who, in spite of certain dramatic talents, had never
been attracted to the stage, she was becoming nervous with
so much public attention, and also bored with the presence
of children around her—although her maternal instincts

could be aroused by men her age or older, with whom she could be most patient and most kind. She was even prepared to be her most generous self with George Cramer—short of knocking him down, she'd certainly given out signals enough for any man—but when one day simply followed another without event, she began to think more kindly of Cyril, like a shipwrecked sailor watching a retreating sail on the horizon.

She'd married Cyril when she was sixteen and he was forty-five. God knows how old that made him now, but he'd been like a father to her and nothing else for the past ten years. She'd thought he was simply incapable of *that* kind of feeling any more, until one evening last May when she'd gotten the shock of a lifetime. . . .

They were in the sitting room, cozy as could be, Cyril in his favorite leather chair and she moving about, plumping up cushions because she always had to be stirring or die. She was relaxed, though, and so popped out with something she didn't even know was in her mind.

"I guess you'd look more lively if Myra was here, old boy."

Why she'd said the name of her own best friend she could not imagine, unless it was from that sixth sense which always told her what people didn't expect her to know. You could have knocked her over with a feather when Cyril put down his book and calmly said: "I hadn't any idea you knew about Myra and me, Ruby. We've never wanted to hurt you, you know."

Naturally Ruby couldn't stay on in Capetown after that. Fortunately, a friend at the shipping office was able to find her a cabin on Captain Jimmy's ship, which, by a strange coincidence, was stocked with soft mattresses, black caviar and vintage champagne, and, though she'd bawled like a baby at first, Captain Jimmy was a man who knew enough about women, so that—as he said later—it hadn't blinded him a bit to her real attractions.

Ruby hadn't been at the pension long before everyone forgot what had interested them before she came. Professor Cook complained that the atmosphere in Paris this summer was not as conducive to work as in other years, but his wife noticed he was always on time now for his meals. Often when Ruby and George lingered in the hall after lunch the Professor was hovering somewhere near these two bright birds of paradise like a dark, long-beaked raven awaiting his turn at the feast.

But the woman had eyes only for George, and the pension bachelor seemed ripe too for just what she seemed to be offering. It was rumored he'd had an unfortunate marriage annulled back in the States, and now had a fiancée in Rome. True or not, he stared at Ruby when he thought no one was looking, in a way which indicated that, if the fiancée actually did exist, she'd better not stay in Rome much longer.

Then one day after a long and earnest conversation in the hall with George, Ruby danced away with such a lingering, excited smile that those who saw her knew things must be coming to a head. Amanda Cook, who had never before seen two such glamorous and sophisticated persons in the very act of falling in love, felt a bit like cheering, as when one's team has made first down at a football game. When George Cramer came back to speak to Amanda she smiled at him in congratulation; it quite surprised her to see the oddly worried look in his eyes.

"Mrs. Cook," he said. "I need your help." Then with his big hand enclosing her thin responsive arm he drew her into a corner and proposed that she and the professor come on an outing with him and the lady from South Africa that Friday night. His invitation was so urgent that Amanda, baffled as she was, decided that Professor Cook would have to give up the Illumination of Nefertiti at the Louvre with whom he'd been promising himself a date.

Unfortunately she had no chance to face her husband with this decision before dinner that night, for as soon as they sat down Professor Cook and Ruby began talking of things they were going to do separately, having no idea plans had been made for them to set out together.

"Tomorrow night Mr. Cramer and I are dining on the *Bateaux-Mouches*, Mademoiselle," Ruby announced, her large shapely body shifting about happily in her chair.

"I've missed Nefertiti every Friday evening she's been lighted," Professor Cook was complaining to Count Gronsky on his left. "Now at last I'm going to see her in all her glory!"

George leaned forward, his blond coloring only slightly more vivid than usual. "Ruby, it's all set. Mrs. Cook and the Professor would *love* to come along with us on the boat. We'll have a ball together, a real *ball,* you know. It's so much more fun in a party!"

The woman from South Africa became still as though held at dead center of a hurricane, and in her eyes was the cold light of a storm. "That's out of the question," she said after a moment's pause. "I told you to reserve a table just for two."

"Amanda, you have forgotten, I think, that *I* am going to the Louvre!" Professor Cook said to his wife with an astonished air. But Amanda fastened on him such a fierce look of contradiction (the truth having dawned on her, that George Cramer wasn't nearly as smitten as the lady would have liked) that he was subdued to silence, and Mademoiselle du Coeur nodded sagely as though she alone understood what was going on.

*   *   *

The lady from Capetown was a stunning sight when they met in the pension's prim little salon at 6:25 the next evening. Mademoiselle, like an amused spectator at the Comédie Française, smiled indulgently on Mr. Cramer pacing nervously from door to window and back, and on the Cooks, sitting squeezed together on the salon's narrow love seat, in evening clothes slightly creased from being put away so long. The boy Julian sprawled on the window seat, staring at Brigitte Bardot on the front page of *Paris-Match*, and several other guests were waiting for the dinner bell, when Ruby came in like an entry at Longchamp curried and polished for the Grand Prix.

She wore an orange chiffon dinner dress, a tiny mink cape over bare shoulders, diamonds at her white throat and pink ears worth a murder on a Paris street—with half an effort anyone could believe the heels of her black satin pumps were real jewels, too—while every line of her sleek excited body proclaimed a winner.

"Oh!" exclaimed Amanda Cook. "How beautiful you look!"

Julian pursed his lips in a soundless wolf whistle, and George Cramer, youthful in gray flannels, bowed low from the waist. When he looked up again his eyes were glazed as if temporarily blinded by a light.

"*La belle dame de la nuit*," he murmured, and Ruby's bright lavender eyes looked pleased as punch with the impression she knew she had made.

"Will I do?" she asked, coyly.

"You look like a splendid hibiscus," asserted the professor, who finally had a chance to use the word fluttering in his mind.

"*Allons-y!*" cried George, offering his arm to Ruby and then sweeping her out the door.

"*Allons-y!*" echoed the Professor, he and Amanda following the handsome pair down the stairs and into a taxi with the top open for the lights of Paris to shine upon their faces.

When they arrived at the dock below place de l'Alma, a long line of diners waited to board the sight-seeing boat, but George Cramer swept Ruby past them all, informing the maître d'hôtel that they had reserved a table, that they were in need of champagne, and that the night air was chilly out here for the ladies. After one look at Ruby the maître seated them by a choice window and presented the wine card to George with a Gallic flourish.

With a voluptuous movement, the gaily lighted excursion boat slowly started up the Seine as Amanda Cook looked contentedly through multiple glasses of champagne at the fascinating, changing face of the river under the stars and lights. At the beginning she had accepted one of Ruby's long dark South African cigarettes, and urged at once, "Call me Amanda." The Professor, after accepting a cigarette himself, although he rarely smoked, conceded with dignity, "You may call me Henry." But Ruby, even as the evening went on, never seemed to say any name but "George."

"Look, George," she'd exclaim as the great white abutments and arches of the narrow flat-topped bridges went past the moving finger of the searchlight of the boat. "George, did you see *that?*"

The other diners seemed unnaturally quiet in contrast to Ruby and George and, finally, to the Professor himself. While Amanda felt, with the air caressing the back of her neck gently as a sigh, that all four of them were part of a romantic past.

"Henry, don't you feel like de Maupassant, drifting on the river Seine?" she asked, her tipsiness only slightly apparent to herself. "And I—I feel like a model of Manet's picnicking on the river banks—" She was not prepared for

George Cramer's sudden laughter which roared out beyond the white oblong of their table.

"Ruby, our Amanda feels like a nude model of Manet's! This is priceless!" But Ruby, who had obviously been trying to hold George's hand under the table, did not seem amused at all.

The tour was over too soon when they left the boat to walk along the quai, the Cooks ahead with Amanda clinging to Henry's arm. Henry had quite taken her breath away with the things he had said, the champagne he had been able to consume, and the fact that they were having an evening like this at all. George and Ruby lingered somewhere behind in the dark, no doubt kissing at last, and Amanda felt not a breath of censure in her heart. Paris, she'd always heard, was for lovers.

"Professor," called George, close behind them, and the Professor stopped as at the voice of a colleague on the campus at home. "Wait a sec!" And they looked around to see George drawing a visibly reluctant Ruby along the stony quai.

"Stop pulling me, George," Ruby was protesting. "My shoes hurt when you pull me like that."

"But I simply must tell the Professor something amusing," said George, and the Professor waited patiently. Amanda felt quite put out.

"Let them go," protested Ruby. "I'm tired of so many people." Amanda, at this moment, could very well see what Ruby meant.

All around them in the dim corners were couples leaning together, walking in rhythmic closeness or kissing, lost to the rest of the world. Soft air from the river blew across their brows, and stars were bright and winking overhead. It was a night for love, for intimacy with the one you loved—

Men can be stupid, Amanda thought, idly noticing how a searchlight from the next riverboat swept like a pointing finger to their corner of the quai.

"I say, look there!" cried Ruby, suddenly coming to life and pointing to two forms lying not far away linked together in the way best known to animals and men. Brought out of the shadows like a print from a negative, this couple was actively engaged in ravishing each other, and Amanda Cook was scarcely able to avert her own eyes quickly enough.

"The beast with two backs! What a sight, George!" Ruby cried joyfully. "Oh, these jolly, jolly French!"

For just an instant Amanda caught sight of George's face before the spotlight passed from it, although it was hard to know what was mirrored there. "Ruby, you naughty girl," he protested, weakly, at the same time taking tight hold of Amanda's arm. Then the spotlight passed altogether, leaving the lovers buried in the night—and a long sigh seemed to escape from George's lips, although he did not let go of Amanda's arm.

"I sometimes think you've got badness on the brain, Ruby," he said, the next moment, cheerily enough, while the Professor stared at Ruby without speech, which, thought Amanda in irritation, was just what George should now be doing, but he could not seem to stop chattering. "Amanda," said George, "you really must not pay any attention to the things this girl says or does, you know. Actually, she's got a fine devoted husband back home, and she misses him like the devil. She's just trying to shock people, that's all. Tell us about Cyril, Ruby. Is he an Englishman of the old school type, or more rugged—a lion hunter, maybe?"

It took Amanda a moment to see that Ruby's head had reared back as though she had been physically struck. When she suddenly and furiously stamped her foot at George, Amanda felt she too would have found it the only thing to do.

"I never heard anything so absolutely prying in my life, George Cramer!" cried Ruby, looking fantastically beautiful under the quai lights. Her hair had come out of its usual sleek shape and the planes of her face were beautiful in a symmetry uncommon these days. Her orange gown curled in the river breeze like the petals of a tropical flower, and the Professor stared in the way he did when absorbed in something beautiful and rare in a museum.

But, swearing under her breath, Ruby raced away on her tottering, glittering heels and rapidly began mounting the steps away from them to the street embankment above.

"Ruby, wait!" George called, nervous as one who has, until now, no idea his fooling has gone too far. "Wait, wait for me, dear," he begged, bounding after her, pursuing her at last. But she kept going, which pleased Amanda, until finally, halfway to the top of the steps, he caught and held the woman in a close and passionate embrace. In the moonlight, Amanda could see them clearly entwined for a long and exciting moment before George broke away at last and called down, quite tremulously, to the Professor.

"There's a magnificent view of the city from here, Professor. Come up and look," he begged, compelled even then, poor man, to include the others. But now even Ruby, almost languidly, waved down to them.

The night seemed more charged than ever with excitement, as they walked gaily in search of a taxi. Ruby clung to George's arm, but he, never one to keep serious for long, began singing *Boola, Boola* at the top of his voice and the Professor joined in, the two of them like college boys marching along the cours la Reine shadowed by the blackest night. Even Ruby, whose feet wobbled on the cobblestones in her ridiculous shoes, laughed and swayed on George's arm and didn't complain one bit.

But finally Amanda felt Henry's steps slow down, and his voice sagged on a high baritone note. It would not be fair if he were so tired now that he would go to sleep the moment his head touched the pillow! Then he pinched her behind wickedly through the thin silk dress and she bubbled with laughter, thinking he would not, after all, wish to sleep immediately tonight.

Back at the pension, as George pushed the button and the sleepy head of the concierge thrust grumpily for one instant from her window, the Professor propelled Amanda rapidly through the entrance. There, briskly shaking hands with George, he led her upstairs like an eager boy, closing their door firmly against all possible interruptions. From the salon on the floor below they could hear Mlle du Coeur's piano, which she sometimes played late at night, and it seemed impossibly romantic to Amanda that in accompaniment to Henry's love-making the strains of The Moonlight Sonata sweetened the midnight air.

Not long after this, however, they both heard George come up alone and enter his bedroom, hurriedly locking the door behind him. There had been no other footsteps, no whispers in the hall; and Amanda was unaccountably disappointed. No matter how proper a woman she might have been all the other nights of her life, tonight was different, and she did think that under such a spell even the lady from the Cape of Good Hope was entitled to her share of happiness.

Ruby Fairlie stared at her image in the wardrobe mirror next morning searching for the unknown enemy. She looked not a day older, did she?—yet her color was unnaturally high in both cheeks as though she had been slapped,

which, in a way, she had been. At the very moment of sur-
render last night, when she had turned to George with her
lips moist and excitement coursing through her veins,
George had been struck by a sharp and unforgivable recall
of memory and had stepped almost brusquely from her
arms!

"Oh, Lord, Ruby, my friend from Rome!—I just
thought, I didn't leave any message with Mam'selle tonight
that this friend might arrive. Now there she is playing the
piano—she must have had some word! I've got to *see* Mam'-
selle, dear—*good*-night. It's been a grand evening, and I've
loved every minute of it. Oh, *do* you suppose my friend
has come while I've been out?"

"I don't see—" Ruby began, then broke off abruptly.
"At this hour? You think someone is up there now in your
room?"

George looked startled and answered, sternly, "Not in my
room, Ruby. Good heavens, what would Mam'selle think?"

So it was a girl, or he wouldn't say a thing like that—
And he had gone running off to Mlle du Coeur, leaving
Ruby standing out there in the hall with her heart racing,
her body aching with tenderness and ready to forget the
world in his arms. . . .

She was angry, for no man ever before had been able to
reject her, in her own top form, but she was also capable of
self-criticism as she peered into her mirror before going
crossly to the window, and there was the broad back of
George himself, fleeing across the courtyard. Still, he was
handsome, so buoyant in his movements, so virile in his
great body that even now, in the bright morning light,
Ruby felt the faintness of desire. At least, last night, one
thing was certain, no girl had come. . . .

As always, her mind could change quickly when her feelings were aroused; so, once again, she started to plan, for

herself, of course, but also for George, who could not possibly know what was right for him. He was a conventional man and she would have to show him there was nothing to lose, tell him how she had been treated by Cyril and how she was ready to divorce him—in other words, lean on George's sympathy, show she was really a good sort who had been injured by those she'd trusted. They could start a new life together—

For a moment, however, Ruby felt a bit weepy thinking of her garden in Capetown which she might never see again. And there was the Captain she would have to forget also if she settled finally for somebody like George. Well, some said if you could stand Jo'burg you could stand anyplace, even America; and with George she'd forget the past even if it had been dear in many ways.

The morning's mail was shoved under her door just as Ruby decided to buy tickets for a play that night, to show George how serious she could be. Absently opening the flap of a letter from Capetown, she thought the Odeon would be just right.—"*Ruby, dear,*" she read; it was from Myra, who was no friend of hers. "*Please don't tear this letter up just because it's from me*—(As if one's curiosity would let one do a thing like that!) "*—and understand I am speaking not only in sorrow for myself but for Cyril, whom each of us, in her own fashion, loves.*"

Well, Ruby was in no mood to be reminded of sorrow, now. She had suffered enough; and for an instant in her mirror the beautiful lips went flat with depression. Like a nun's, she thought in sudden alarm, taking up her lipstick and going over their curves until she looked herself again. No, she simply was not reading that letter, now.

She would dress, she decided, walking briskly, across the Park, in quiet dignity: for tonight her whole appearance must be calculated to show George, the timid, what he was

missing without a woman like herself at his side. Then she
bought two tickets, the last in a row—George could not
bring the Cook's in on that excursion!—and back at the
pension for lunch, she left them in his mail slot with a note:
*"We were all a bit giddy last night, weren't we? How about
a nice sober evening at the theater for a change, if your
'friend' hasn't come?"*
Then through lunch she remained so quiet that George
looked quite anxious by the time she excused herself early
and went up to her room.

That evening the Professor and Amanda had a quiet dinner at the pension, suffering from hangovers but frequently
holding hands during the meal. They had noticed Ruby and
George go out earlier, saying they would dine in the neighborhood of the theater. Ruby was dressed in a plain black
dress and pearls with the mink cape, her eyes clear and
bright and her step light as ever, while George wore a dark
navy suit in which he might have been going to offer con-
dolences to a friend. Amanda wondered if they would be
able to stay up so late again, feeling no envy but a fleeting
regret that there would be no more extravagant parties with
these two for herself and the Professor; she must depend
on simpler pleasures after this—the only kind the Professor
could afford on his Fellowship.
After dinner they went directly to their room, Henry
settling down to work at the small table, saying after an
hour that at last he'd managed to get a little concentrated
work done. By ten-thirty he turned out the light on his
side of the bed with a sigh of satisfaction, and everything
seemed as it was meant to be. Then, just as Amanda was
about to fall asleep he said, unexpectedly, "I'd certainly
hate to be married to that woman. In spite of certain—ah,

charms, Amanda, I want you to understand that her appeal was, for me—ah, only *phy*sical."

Sleep left Amanda's brain and for an instant alarm filled in. "I—guess I didn't know, Henry," she said, leaning up on her elbow and looking down at the solemn outline of her husband's face. "I guess I didn't understand—Thank you for telling me."

His big angular hand patted her shoulder gently. "When you think of the life such a woman must have had— After all, last night, we did put on quite a *ball*." He paused to savor the new word. "Yet there she is, taking poor Cramer out again tonight, never thinking she might just stay in sensibly, like this."

"I think we've had a lovely evening too, dear," said Amanda, falling back on her pillow, and after that there was a companionable silence between them until they dozed off, side by side.

They were awakened by a rude and curious commotion in the hall, although it was hard to tell right off what it was. Then they heard the excited whispering voices of George and Ruby and, to Amanda's horror and delight, the Professor popped out of bed to open their door a crack so they could hear the voices quite distinctly.

"George, you silly thing, he's an old man, I tell you. He doesn't even *care* what I do, I swear it—Oh, George—" After all, a woman with impulses like Ruby's couldn't speak softly if she tried, although the momentary richness of her voice was something of a revelation to Amanda, as it may have been to the Professor.

"Ruby, you naughty girl! I tell you, dear, we'd both regret—" Then the whispering was suddenly cut off and they could hear heavy breathing and, the next moment, a giggle from Ruby and a gasp from George. "Ruby, you mustn't, must *not*, girl—Oh, Ruby, I can't stand that!" And for a moment there was another silence in the hall which did not mean the absence, as anyone must know, of amorous activity.

The Professor was nodding sagely in the moonlight, a wicked, participating approval in his eyes. He was even about to close the door when suddenly they heard running footsteps on the stairs, and then the sharp, shrill, questioning voice of Mlle du Coeur.

"Ah, good evening, Mr. Cramer. Good evening, Madame —How was the theater? Good, eh? Very difficult play, *Port Royal*, I think, but stimulating, *n'est-ce pas?*"

Now they could hear George answer Mademoiselle in such a nervous high voice it hardly sounded like his own; Ruby, it seemed, was stricken, unable to say a word.

"*Pardon*," Mlle du Coeur went on. "Mr. Cramer, I have the new keys you request for your door. It is late, yes, but I did not remember to try them in the day. Please, we see now?" And the Cooks heard the brisk, determined movements of the Frenchwoman in front of George Cramer's door where she tried the keys, seemingly hundreds of them, the tiny clink of metal against metal going on far into the night.

At lunch next day Ruby's place was set, her half-filled wine bottle before it as though she were expected, but she was not there. George came in pale and nervous, to shove bits of food about on his plate with an abstracted air, and said nothing to anyone.

Mlle du Coeur, who glanced at him from time to time with concern, asked pleasantly "And do you expect your friend from Rome to arrive very soon, Mr. Cramer?"

George's brows drew together as though his private thoughts had been interrupted. "No. Well, that is—I may decide to drift on down toward Rome, instead," he said, as though it had been necessary to search his memory for an answer.

"We shall be sorry to lose you, Mr. Cramer. It is a pity that your friend cannot come here."

"He likes it there, I guess," said George, without enthusiasm. "He's a painter, you know. Light, and all that—"

"The light of Paris is very good, also," Mademoiselle reminded him, without rancor. "Perhaps you will bring him to us later?" Amanda, idly listening to this conversation, suddenly sat up. Why, they were talking about a "him" after all . . .

That afternoon on her way from the American Express Amanda passed the Café de la Paix and there sat Ruby alone and solemn at a street-side table.

"Hello," called Ruby. "Come join me, won't you? I'm feeling blue—Did you know I'm taking the plane home tonight?"

"Oh, I am sorry," said Amanda, sincerely, for Ruby Fairlie had been something of an experience. Besides, she always felt regret at the moment of leaving anyone. "Is it unexpected?" she asked.

Ruby's slanted violet eyes brooded out over the Place de l'Opéra. "It's unexpected, all right. My husband is dying."

"How dreadful!" The full drama of the situation swept over Amanda in a superstitious wave as she thought, while Ruby was out with George Cramer, that's what was in store for her! "I'm so sorry," she said, hoping Ruby hadn't guessed the turn her thoughts had taken.

"Well, it wasn't the news I thought I'd get," said Ruby. "What will you drink? Mine's Pernod. It's best for the nerves, I think."

"I'll have Pernod, too," said Amanda, bravely. "Your husband—was he a young man?"

"Lord no, he's old enough to die. But I'll miss the old boy."

If there weren't tears in Ruby's eyes, at least her face looked almost as any other woman's might, bearing such news. "I thought he was carrying on with my own best friend," she said, then took a long, sighing drink from her glass. "Myra says he wasn't, now—She could be telling the truth. He was a real gentleman, you know," she added, as one speaking already of the dead.

Then unexpectedly she looked straight into Amanda's face. "Did anyone ask for me at lunch?" she asked. "Did George Cramer say anything to Mam'selle?"

"He hardly spoke at all," Amanda remembered. "Or ate much either—"

"*Garçon, la même chose*—Well, I left him a note this morning, told him why I had to leave—" Ruby's expression had become very earnest. "George Cramer is a gentleman, too, you know!"

Amanda nodded, feeling she was holding a tea-cup for Ruby to fill with the heady brew of her confidences.

"I'm sure I never thought he wasn't," she said, encouragingly.

"If you could have heard the things he said to me last night," said Ruby, and Amanda had the grace to blush. "We've been—well, friendly, you know," Ruby went on, pouring again. "I guess I'm just naughty enough to think we might have come to an understanding—until he said what he did."

Amanda waited, not daring to guess what this was.

"Do you know that George told me he never had and he never would lay a finger on a married woman? Imagine that!"

"Imagine!" echoed Amanda faintly but with sympathy

wondering, with a sophistication she had not known she possessed, what could be the matter with George.

"I couldn't believe him at first—it almost seemed like an excuse, somehow. Until I finally had to admit that I just never had known such a gentleman before."

Amanda nodded approvingly, wishing this fascinating conversation would never end.

"Then when I found out about this girl in Rome, you can fancy how I felt."

Amanda suddenly stirred. "Ruby, you're wrong about that—there is no girl in Rome!" she said excitedly. "It *is* a man, just as he said. He was talking to Mademoiselle about him at lunch!"

For an instant Ruby looked startled, and she took a quick, thirsty drink from her glass, the smooth white skin creasing between the dark beautiful brows and the bright gleaming lips straightening the voluptuous curves that made Ruby's beauty what it was. "Well—what do you know!"

There was only one thing in the world Amanda cared about at that moment, and this was to hear what Ruby would say next. "A man, Ruby," she repeated. "Just an artist man friend—"

Ruby looked thoughtfully and then with awakening interest into her glass as her brow cleared, and this time, the drink she took was long and unhurried and deep. Finally, she set the glass down and turned an unexpectedly mischievous, not at all convincing look of grief on Amanda Cook. "God rest Cyril's soul," she said piously, as though already placing a coffin lid over his face. "He'll be dead before I can get there anyway."

Somehow it did not surprise Amanda to see George Cramer striding down the Boulevard the next moment, or for him to turn into the café as though on appointed time. "I got your note," he said, a troubled new light of uncertainty in his eyes. "I couldn't let you go, Ruby, not without saying good-bye—"

"I'm not married any more, George," she said simply. "Now do sit down—"

Amanda, forgotten, excused herself politely. She could now tell Henry and Mademoiselle that Ruby Fairlie had found the key to George's heart, at last; and even if she were not there to see George's face when Ruby seized his hands and held them as though never again to let him go, it did not matter. The next moment he relaxed as one finally within sight of land in a previously uncharted sea.

Summer of a Dead Hero

On a day toward the end of July when the heat held Paris in a close and stifling embrace, Julian smelled Friday's fish cooking on the pension stove and a quiver started in his stomach. He said nothing of this to his mother, but now it seemed that all the wasted hours of this seventeenth summer of his life were descending on him like an illness. He was bored, he would rather be at home with his friends, swimming, playing tennis, seeing girls; he hated Paris, and when he got home the summer would be ended.

Mildred could see well enough how it was, with Julian's wrists hanging like plucked birds and his body elongating right before her eyes. When Mlle du Coeur, the owner of the pension, remarked that the boy's color was green as unripe fruit Mildred helplessly agreed, but what could she do about it? She'd brought the boy abroad on impulse, never guessing that Paris could be the worst possible choice for an adolescent boy and for his mother (who'd hoped to have some diversion of her own) during the summer months. So when the Frenchwoman spoke of a widow of good family

34

near Mont-Saint-Michel who sometimes accepted young persons away from the city and the summer heat, Mildred listened hopefully, and wrote Mme Devereux with only faint misgivings.

"Julian needs the sea air for his liver," said Mlle du Coeur. "If his lungs were in danger, the Alps, naturally, would be preferred. But—" here the face of the Frenchwoman rounded with a tender smile "—for the 'green sickness,' who can tell?"

Mildred, feeling some embarrassment with her understanding of what the Frenchwoman meant, was greatly relieved when, by return mail, the letter came accepting Julian (and two hundred francs, or a little more than forty dollars a week) for his remaining time in France.

Julian was put on a train for St. Pierre-de-la-mer the twenty-seventh of July which fell on a Thursday, thus avoiding the weekend traveling crowds, and Mildred bought oranges and candy from a platform vendor, chattering unceasingly to keep him from seeing her apprehensions and herself from feeling an obscure sense of guilt. After all, he spoke French better than she did.

"Those lessons you've been having with Madame Oreilles have done wonders for your accent, darling. Now use your French often," she urged, standing at the door of the second-class carriage as the French occupants stared with frank amusement at this full-grown American boy with the nervous, chattering mother.

"I'll get along," he mumbled, wishing she would leave. Any dope could see she wasn't making him very popular with these French people, standing there in her fancy silk dress and big shiny handbag that made her look too rich, too American. He tried to make himself smaller in his seat.

"Did we pack your bathing trunks?" she asked suddenly

in exaggerated concern. "Oh, Julian, I can't remember! And they'll be the very *first* things you'll need!" She even looked up at his suitcase on the rack overhead as though she'd take it down and open it right there in front of everyone.

"You packed them," he reminded her, tersely.

Knowing she was embarrassing him, certain she'd said all there was to say, still she could not stop; for in spite of the twice-weekly shave and deepening voice, Julian was still a child. She'd heard that French boys were appallingly sophisticated, and as for French girls, who were said to mature at an age when American children were still playing with dolls, it was frightening to think what he might learn from them.

Fortunately, a warning "beep" sounded outside and Mildred had to step out of the train. With her last sight of the boy's thin, pale face and brighter than usual eyes, she could do no more than remind herself that Julian's father had said the boy must be given some independence (from his mother) this summer and that six weeks, surely, could not corrupt a boy. Yet it took two brandies and four cigarettes on the terrace of the Café de la Paix before she could look around again and begin to enjoy life as other American women on holiday seemed to be doing.

Once the train was speeding through the countryside, an elderly French lady began talking to Julian. As he couldn't understand much that she said, he pretended to be interested in the landscape racing past his window. He was feeling uneasy anyhow, both in his stomach and in his mind; so when she offered him a small loaf of crusty bread he accepted it, nibbling on the crust the way kids did in France. He found it surprisingly good. Then the old lady went to sleep with her head tipped to one side while the three other French people in the compartment chattered on loud as ever and pointed out to him places of interest. Once they showed the remains of bombed buildings, saying *"Les Américains,"* and explaining with only a shade of reproach, *"pour la libération!"*

Finally, it was time for lunch and the French people—all but the old lady, who was asleep—began bringing out their lunches. Julian went to the diner, where he did pretty well ordering an omelette and milk, jotting down in his notebook: eight francs. Then he went back to the compartment and watched more Normandy cows and villages go by until suddenly the old lady woke up and pointed to the north.

"The Channel is there," she said, in perfect English, which didn't seem to him quite fair. But there at last was a glimpse of the sea, which seemed to make everyone feel good, and they all bowed and smiled and told him to have a good vacation as the train pulled into the Dinard station, dumped him, and then pulled out again.

He was alone on the platform—no, there was one other boy, a little kid wearing horn-rimmed glasses and abbreviated shorts who was being approached by a slim, blonde woman in a white dress and green sweater. The kid stared at her and shook his head vigorously, so then Julian guessed this was Mme Devereux looking for him.

"Maybe you're looking for me," he said, walking up to her. *"Je suis* Julian Hadley," he tried as she turned quickly to face him.

"Mais non! But you are a young man," she exclaimed in English, her blue eyes wide with astonishment. "I look for *little* boy."

"That's okay," he said, naturally flattered. "I'm sure glad you speak English, though, Mme Devereux."

"I live two year in England as a girl," she said, continuing to examine him, not unpleasantly. "So you are American boy. Julian—but that is French name? Tell me, are you strong? Do you like to swim in the sea?"

"Swimming's my best sport," he admitted, modestly.

"*Bon!* We will swim together in the mornings. From the rocks, behind the house," she promised, then reached for his suitcase which he swung away from her just in time. He even bounced it a bit as he followed her to the car, although it was heavy enough, filled with all the things his mother had made him bring: books he was supposed to read, too many clothes, and the candy for Mme Devereux, which now he was glad he'd brought.

The small pink face of a little girl, her eyes brown and bright, peered from the window of an old gray Citroën. Two dimpled hands were held out in welcome.

"*Es-tu Julian? Je m'appelle Suzanne!*" Then the pretty child began chanting, "Julian, Julian, Julian," making little bird calls of his name as she squeezed against her mother to make room for him in the front seat. As they drove off she examined his features solemnly as though he were a tree on which she would build a nest.

By the time they crossed the spit of land to the village of St. Pierre, Julian was talking as he'd not done all summer; and when Mme Devereux pointed out her big yellow house sitting like a hen in the midst of trees and fields with the blue Channel rippling out beyond, it needed only the stout, blue-aproned Breton maid smiling from the door in welcome to make Julian feel he'd found a new home.

Early next morning Mme Devereux called from beneath his window. He looked out to see her in a white toweling beach robe, pushing her light hair up under a bathing cap, and even at this distance her eyes were a bright astonishing blue. She seemed younger than on the day before.

"Oh, gee, is it late?" he exclaimed, batting the sleep from his eyes.

"Ah, *non*. It is only seven. But the tide goes out early today. We swim now if you come quick."

He backed so fast into the room he bumped his head on the raised sash, but in two minutes he had on his orange swimming trunks and was racing after Mme Devereux on the grass path leading toward the water. She paused, apparently amused by his thin legs white as roots long buried in the earth, but when he tripped she did not laugh; she did shake her head warningly.

"Careful, please," she cautioned him. "The path is steep. We do not want you to fall, spinning like a rock into the water!"

When they reached the edge of the cliff he could see what she meant. Far below, the sea's white foam and spray slapped against the elephantine gray sides of a natural boat basin, and there was a narrow path down which they must make their way. He followed her on the precipitous trail with his heart unsteady, but the instant they reached the water he felt fine. Out on the horizon, small fishing boats bobbed like playful kittens, birds sang high in the trees far above, and fleecy clouds in the blue sky were guileless as the face of Suzanne. Mme Devereux plunged at once into the sea, where her long white arms spread in a breast-stroke strong as his own crawl. But she was heading straight out toward an island maybe two miles away and expected him to follow!

The water was cold as a winter lake, but her white cap, like a big headless duck, kept right on. Julian began to lose ground, yet he could not stop, did not know what else to do until she turned and swam back toward him, straightening two yards away and sinking up to her nose. Then she lifted both arms to show she touched bottom. His heart was beating regularly again when she called, "Put your feet down here, Julian. See how the tide goes quick now, like I tell you?"

He stretched his stiff, chilled limbs just far enough to touch sand and still keep his head clear, feeling an enormous and instant relief.

"I wasn't sure how much longer I could hold out," he admitted. "I'm out of practice, I guess."

"You boys get cold too quick," she said, smiling as drops of water trickled from her white cap down over her long fine nose. "We must make more flesh on your bones with Catharine's good soup."

He grinned and turned to look over the distance they had covered from the land. It was then he noticed a big black rock rising not a dozen feet away, no part of which had been in sight the moment before, and then other rocks rising to left and right like warriors suddenly sprung from the sea. "I never saw anything like that before!" he exclaimed.

"One must not be caught on these rocks when the tide is rising," she said, swimming now on her back. "The tide goes out fast, but it comes in very fast also. There is danger."

"I can see that," he said, diving down to the sandy bottom, clasping both arms under his knees and whirling his body about in a wild, splashy somersault. Opening his eyes to all he could see on the floor below, he rose and dived again, swimming under water a moment or so. The water seemed safe and friendly now as on other summers of his life—but when he rose to the surface he saw that the undertow had carried him well beyond the point where he had been. Quickly he swam back over the distance which separated him from Mme Devereux.

"You have heard of Mont-Saint-Michel?" she asked. "It is there, a great monastery, like an island at high tide. And far, far away, over there, is England." He could see how her eyes, for an instant, lingered on the horizon. "We go back now," she said, her mood suddenly changing, and Julian followed her toward shore where the purple rocks now fully exposed were perforated with small caves. Octopi, she told him, hid there; and Julian was engulfed by a sense of adventure as he thought of this and of the tides, and of the kindness of Mme Devereux.

Suzanne came running down the path in her long white nightgown, and the mother caught the child in her arms, making a picture, Julian thought: they were pretty as any picture. Then something else stirred in his heart, leaving an oddly surprised feeling of his own size and strength. He thought then that if he had to, he could take care of them, at least for as long as he was there.

It was on the second morning that another ritual began, or rather Julian was initiated into an already existing one. The child tried to tell him about this, her round pink arms gesturing toward the sea.

"*Papa, là,*" she said pointing. "*Là, Julian. Venez avec moi!*"

"*Papa, là?*" he asked, and the child nodded excitedly.

"Suzanne speaks of my husband, who is buried near the rocks," Mme Devereux explained quietly. "Maurice Devereux was a hero of the Résistance. The villagers, they demand that he be buried here, where he was loved."

"A hero of the War?" asked Julian, in surprise.

"*Oui.* And of the peace." She looked a little stern as she said this. "Would you like to go with us? It is green—the villagers keep it so."

Even if he did not know what to expect, he was curious. Who would expect to find a hero's grave out here? "Sure," he said. "*Oui*—I'd like to go."

Suzanne gathered blossoms growing half-wild around the house and led the way along a wooded path to the rocks where the sea could be seen for a great distance, dark water against the lighter blue of the sky. Then when she pointed, he saw the grave, a plain, sod-covered mound with a small wooden cross at its head, a bunch of half-wilted violets at its base. Was this all? It was so humble! Nothing about this grave suggested any glory, a hero's death.

Yet when Mme Devereux and Suzanne crossed themselves, kneeling and bowing their heads, Julian thought, if I'd known him I bet I'd feel the way they do. And indeed, something of the combination of sea and silence and the small brave kneeling figures stirred him unexpectedly.

Suzanne gravely put the fresh blossoms on the cross as her mother tossed the wilted ones over the rocks onto the shore below.

"The villagers still come—but not as before," she said. "They still believe Maurice belongs to them, you know." There was a small bitterness in her voice that Julian heard but did not understand. "More than to me," she added quietly.

The child looked briefly anxious and Julian said quickly, "Gosh, it must be great to be a hero!"

"It is better to be alive, I think," said Mme Devereux. "It is enough. Now we go." But as they started back toward the house, she asked, "You would like to know about heroes, eh, young American?"

"I sure would!"

"Then I tell you about Maurice. They took him from his printing press, the Nazis, and they shot him down against a wall. Someone he trusted had betrayed him." Her chin lifted and for an instant she turned to stare brightly in his eyes. "He died laughing in their faces."

The child clapped her plump small hands, and Julian expelled a long, incredulous breath. "He laughed at them? *Wow!*"

The American expression fell so oddly on the summer air that Mme Devereux seemed startled, and quickly lowered her white chin, reaching out a hand for the child. "Come," she said. "Catharine waits us."

They could see the bright ruddy face of the cook watching from her kitchen window, and as they came closer the smell of chocolate and warm bread stirred Julian's appetite so that he could hardly wait to sit at the table. It was Mme Devereux, that morning, who barely ate a thing.

Daily the companionship between him and the Frenchwoman grew so that he was hardly able to believe his luck in being here. There was always excitement in going out in the cold, changeable sea; she never stopped warning him, though, about the tides.

"Never face danger when it does not prove something," she said, more than once. "One must learn to fear some things." But once she had spoken seriously she would become gay quickly and so young that it hardly seemed natural to call her "Madame," as one would any stranger. Julian simply ceased calling her anything at all until she noticed and reminded him that her name was Anne, and after that he found himself saying first thing in the morning and last thing at night, "Anne. Anne——"

On Sundays they went to early Mass; on Tuesdays and Thursdays and Saturdays they drove to the public market at Dinard, he carrying a basket for heavy objects while Anne dangled a black string bag loosely over her arm until it was filled with things she wanted. She loved bright new pans and dishes and colored towels; and once, holding a length of yellow cotton up under her chin, gathering it in at the waist, she asked, "Tell me, Julian. Does this make me look young, like you?"

He took care to speak judiciously, as his father might do.

"Very much, I think," he assured her. "Yellow is a good color for you, Anne." But she left it on the stand after all, buying instead three pot-holders for Catharine and a blue pinafore for Suzanne.

Suzanne started about this time calling him "Papa Julian," and sometimes Anne did, too, as a joke. *"C'est comme il faut* that we have a papa in the house," she said, "to carry all these heavy things." Then she might add, her head to one side and her blue eyes bright with laughter, *"Mais*—for a papa I think you need more flesh on your bones!"

She and Catharine liked to tease him about this, pinching the hard muscles of his arm, the cook laughing heartily. Afterwards he would lie out on the rocks alone and stare up into the sky thinking contentedly how natural it was to be here with them, and how he hated the cities, all cities, or any other place remote from the sea. He knew how Maurice Devereux must have felt about this, or any soldier would, coming home from war.

Often out there he thought of the dead hero so intensely that sometimes in fact he could imagine himself instead of the Frenchman against that Paris wall. His heart racing in the stillness of a summer's day, he, too, would face the enemy, his eyes open wide and the murderous guns levelled straight at his heart; finally, he, too, would fall . . .

But on other days Julian stood back assuming the role of adjutant to a hero, smartly saluting with his back rigid and his face respectful in the presence of his commanding officer. At such times, he felt a deep, inarticulate loyalty to the soldier in his grave.

Anne wore simple dresses during the day, but for the evening she often dressed in bright peasant style, thin, loose, gypsy blouses falling low on her shoulders and loops of heavy gold earrings on her curving neck. Julian was pleased when she dressed so for him, and for her he dampened and brushed his black hair, now grown long as a French boy's, until it gleamed. Then he and Suzanne would sit in the candle's glow extravagantly admiring Anne, who had a Frenchwoman's way of casting a spell for those she loved, excluding all others outside the boundary of her table, and her life.

Sometimes before they finished dinner the child would lean beside Julian's chair, her sleepy head on his shoulder and her dark eyes with the deep black fringe of lashes drooping, almost closing. Anne smiled on them both, shutting out the past and the future, also, as though from this moment on there could be no change. Then she would give each a very small glass of *cidre* and they would soon after go quietly to their beds.

There were other hours they did not share. Anne, unlike his mother, was never active without cause—no bather in the sun with heavy-scented oils upon her skin and black, distorting glasses on her eyes. Anne, when not actively engaged, lay in the shade of the chestnut tree with her eyes closed and her hands absolutely at rest. When Julian came upon her sleeping like this, a pale, lovely figure unconsciously beautiful, disturbingly woman, he had to struggle against a child's irrational impulse to awaken her, bring her back from a world which shut him out. And sometimes he even thought to arouse her roughly by some gesture of violence, to disturb this dreaming which cast its own spell over the mystery of her face.

It was at the beginning of the third week, after he'd gone to the rocks alone—Anne had been too busy with Suzanne to visit the grave—that he came upon her lying in the coolness of the shade with her eyes closed, her lashes wingshaped on the high golden cheeks, and her lips slightly parted.

As he stared she moved faintly, the stirring of her slender body perhaps no more than a response of nerves to the passing breeze, and yet the young man sensed something subtler, some sensuousness and grace utterly unimagined by him before. There was the mystery rippling through her like an impulse not to be denied, and for a long moment the boy stood scarcely breathing; when the child came out from the house to stare at him in turn, her head tipped thoughtfully to one side and her doll dragging on the ground, he still did not move.

"*Mama*," Suzanne said at last with the smallest, lightest expenditure of breath. "*C'est Julian et moi, ici.*"

For a brief moment, as one reluctant to leave a dream, Anne lay quietly, although she was awake. Then, the muscles of her face barely disturbed by the opening of her blue eyes, she looked up and reached out a hand for the child. "Ah, Suzanne—Julian, you have been staring at me!" she said accusingly. "Did I look silly? Have I been sleeping long?" Then she sat up and smiled on them both. "Oh, isn't it a beautiful day!"

"Suzanne and I could take some flowers to the grave," Julian said harshly, although he had not thought of this the moment before. "We didn't go yesterday," he accused her, not understanding why he suddenly felt so upset. "I go alone when you forget—"

The Frenchwoman sat up slowly, shaking her head. At the moment a streak of sunlight filtered through the leaves to touch her hair. "Ah, *mon chéri*, but you are *très gentil*." And she put her long narrow feet down on the grass. "Come, my children, we will go together to the rocks, to Maurice. Now!"

So again they took the familiar path to the place where the dead hero slept in the summer sun, and Julian, his face

staunch and solemn as a soldier's, stood at full attention behind them while they knelt and prayed.

Anne saw to it that he met Jacques and Michel, fellows
his own age, who took Julian to the public beach where
brightly striped tents like miniature circuses dotted the
sand. The boys were all right, he got along with them, and
their school English was a lot better than his French—and
he learned some dirty words more interesting than those he
already knew. They were smart in other ways, too—although sometimes he retreated from their daring plans as
from their constant smoking of the strong black Caporal
cigarettes.

Together they walked past tents with flaps pinned back
on the sea, hoping to spy some female dressing inside, and
naturally each boy felt a thrill of discovery at the sight of
a bare leg, or arm, or thigh. Their comments then would be
racy and bold, as each tried to sound more a man than the
other, and when one day they saw a boy only a few years
older than themselves embracing with passion an unidenti-
fied woman, before the flap was jerked down in conceal-
ment, they felt equally rewarded, equally dismayed.

Julian saw then that the French boys were no more prepared to put their knowledge into action than he, in spite
of their boasts; yet he stored away for winter use back
home in school their remarks about the things they imagined taking place within that tent. Anne teased him sometimes about his hours with the boys, asking if they had
noticed any pretty girls there on the beach.

"Without doubt, *mon chéri,* the girls have noticed you!"
she challenged him gaily one evening at dinner, and for the
first time poured out for him in the tiny glass an infinitesi-
mal amount of old Calvados. "To your first little love," she

said, and he flushed under her bright encouraging eyes as
he gulped down the hot, strong drops of liquor.

But the girls had noticed them all right. The giggles
which followed after him and his friends when they loped
past like long-legged colts at liberty had a sound like girl's
voices at home; yet different, too, being suddenly shrill,
then low and secret. And they seemed to know the effect
they had, shy and prim one minute and bold the next, delib-
erately stirring the flesh on a boy's skin and excitement in
his blood—although he never did get very close to one of
them, watched over as they were by old women. One girl
had long flying brown hair and wore each day a red bathing
suit. She looked at him and not once at Jacques or Michel,
but she never had a chance to speak because of her old
granny sitting on a little folding chair in the shade of their
tent nearby.

One day when Julian came back from the beach Suzanne
threw herself in his arms, her laughter chirruping on the
summer air, surprising him so they both fell headlong a
short distance away from Anne, who was reading in her
chair. Clumsily he set Suzanne back on her feet; but then
he surprised a curious look on the Frenchwoman's face as
her eyes dwelt on the length of his naked, darkly tanned
legs and his thin, half-exposed body as though she had not
seen him before.

"Aren't you growing, Julian?" she asked, her voice gentle
and amused. "You are truly big like a man, now—and very
handsome, too."

He did not know how to answer, but the next instant she
yawned, raising her arms comfortably above her head and
dropping the book; while beside her the cat blinked and
Suzanne stretched out in the grass and pretended to sleep.
Anne, too, then closed her eyes so they both looked equally

defenseless, equally appealing. And Julian thought suddenly, worriedly, who will take care of Anne and Suzanne after I am gone?

There had been little rain in the mornings, but one day Julian overslept and awoke to a thin gray light across the sky and the smell of rain in the air. He felt a lazy reluctance to leave his bed, and, without hurrying, dressed and went downstairs where Catharine was standing at her stove, her fat arms in motion over her big orange enameled pans.

"Madame has gone to the train," she told him. "Monsieur Raoul arrives today," she announced, as though this were an important event, and indeed the smells and activity coming from the kitchen stove indicated that someone worthy of her best efforts was expected.

The night's rain was ended although the sky was still gray as Julian walked down to the dark wet rocks. But this morning the sea bored him, and he found himself waiting impatiently for Anne's return, depressed that she'd not taken him along, aware of an oddly hollow feeling in the region of his heart.

Back at the house he fretted, sitting for a time in her chair, now damp as was all else left out in the rain. He tried to study his French grammar but even that did not make much sense, now that he had the sound of their speech in his ears. Then he heard her car clattering on to the dirt road, and, wishing that he were young enough to run and meet them, Julian walked with dignity and apparent boredom around the house as the little French car came tossing down the lane.

Anne brought it to a nervous bad stop, and he saw at once the dark, handsome stranger who held Suzanne affectionately on his lap. It was the man who spoke first, a man with something puzzlingly familiar in his face. " 'Allo," he called pleasantly, as Anne pulled on the hand brake. "We have arrived!"

"Hello," said Julian stiffly as they got out of the car. "I wondered if you were ever coming back, Anne." Then he ducked his head in embarrassment as Anne glanced at him with quick concern and she put her arm half about him, saying, "I have been telling my good friend, Raoul, about my good friend, Julian."

Still he had difficulty smiling, entering that circle of good humor which seemed astonishingly to exist without him. Even Suzanne regarded him with greater sophistication than could be justified by her five years.

"Julian is a French name, too," remarked the stranger, conversationally, giving his hand a strong, hard shake. "Anne tells me you are the perfect guest and that, with you, she must swim each morning in *la Manche*. I tell her this is good. She is thus taking some exercize, also."

"She doesn't have to go with me," Julian protested, suddenly feeling an agony of guilt. He'd not once suspected that she might be going just for him, that she might not swim at all when he was not there.

"Raoul considers me a lazy woman," Anne said quickly. "Now tell him it is not true, Julian. We must show him how we are busy, busy, busy all the day."

"Well, I don't think you work so hard," said Julian, and was not prepared for their sudden laughter.

"Ah, M'sieu Raoul!" cried Catharine, wiping her hands on the sides of her white apron before M. Raoul seized her in his arms, and by the affectionate, rapid way they talked together Julian knew the Frenchman was someone she, too, knew well. But when Raoul let Catharine swing his three heavy bags from the back seat of the car Julian thought scornfully that he himself would never have permitted this,

and was tempted to say so when Anne took his arm, leading
them all into her house.

Almost at once things changed. Everyone became
gayer, talked more, and Anne had little time now to rest
with closed eyes and languid air in her garden chair. She
still sat under the tree, but laughingly, to supervise the fe-
verish activity, the improvements that Raoul insisted he and
Julian bring to the grounds about her house. First he cut
back some of the long vines with a scythe, then he set Julian
and Suzanne and even Catharine, at times, to weeding the
border now so long neglected.

"It was beautiful when Maurice was alive," conceded
Anne. And after that they worked clearing the path to the
rocks, hacking out roots and leveling it in spots with sand
and soil.

At other times Raoul and Julian climbed trees around the
house to cut back dead branches and dislodge vines choking
the growth so sunlight could flood the windows of the
downstairs rooms. Everything was an improvement on what
had been, although Julian could not understand one man's
doing so much in another's house, particularly since he had
discovered that the Frenchman was only a paying guest like
himself. One day he had seen him giving money into the
hand of Catharine, no doubt the same amount Julian's
mother paid; somehow he felt better after this.

Anne was still affectionate with him, rumpling his hair
as she came by and holding his arm when the four of them
went out together, letting Suzanne follow with Raoul. She
seemed more relaxed, too, as though there was less to worry
her, so Julian guessed the extra money had been needed.

The daily swim was naturally à trois, although sometimes
now Anne did not bother to rise so early, and then he and
Raoul went alone. Suzanne divided her attentions equally,

even though it was Raoul she attacked first when they returned from town or from the water, calling him "Papa Raoul," as she had once called Julian "Papa Julian"; and often enough Raoul carried Suzanne upstairs to her bed at night, Anne following, her almost wraithlike slim body lost in the shadows of the stairs.

Then early one dawn Julian awoke with Maurice Devereux in his thoughts, and remembered they had not gone to his grave in many days. This so disturbed him that he got out of bed at once and, as the faint light of the early sun pinpointed the cross visible from his upstairs window, he slipped across the dew-wet grass with a troubled sense of injustice. While he and Raoul had altered and improved the home the dead hero had loved, Maurice himself had been forgotten. Even Anne, now so concerned with the living— he remembered sharply her early, gentler expression of sorrows—seemed, in some unfathomable way, too gay, and thus guilty of betrayal.

The grave looked small and insignificant in the pale light of the rising sun. For a moment it did not seem to matter if anyone came, or if it was a hero or a stone buried in this narrow bed. Then the sun unexpectedly brightened on the cross, and Julian threw himself on the mound, soundlessly repentant, his belief in the reality of the hero more intense for his moment of rejection.

When he stood up again the sun was higher and Catharine was moving before the window of the kitchen. He'd go for a swim alone this morning, he decided, since Anne had not come out for several mornings, and he did not feel like seeing Raoul, now.

Standing half decisively between the house and the grave, he looked back and was surprised to see Anne at an upstairs window. For a moment he could not think why it was strange to see her there, until he realized it was not a window in her room, or Suzanne's either, but one he had not thought was used, next to Raoul's, at the other end of the corridor from his own.

Anne vanished, and he was puzzled that she was up so early on that day. Then the thought came to him, hopefully, that she, too, had suddenly remembered the dead hero, although it worried him to recall how sad and dispiritedly she had been staring over his head at the rising tide of the sea.

Julian roamed restlessly with the French boys until Jacques and Michel had to leave for Angers, where they lived. There was no use trying to make new friends now, since his own time was growing short. Besides, when Anne was there, he felt a curious reluctance to leave the house, which he'd not had before. When she went out, as she sometimes did alone with Raoul, he wandered down on the beach hoping to find someone to talk to, and one day he caught a big red ball thrown by the French girl with the long pretty hair. For a while they threw it back and forth in silence, and in perfect understanding of each other's rhythms as the old woman watched from the shadow of her tent but did not stop them. She let the girl play for almost an hour before she called, "Minette," and the girl obediently went away, but not before she'd stared in his eyes a brief moment, a secret smile upon her face.

Saying "Minette" to himself, so he would not forget, Julian ran back to the house for lunch. He felt better than he had for days, but when he again found himself lunching alone—they had taken Suzanne with them this time—he felt depressed.

An hour later the tide was low enough to go out across the wet sands and explore the rocks risen again like animals from sleep. In places the sea had disappeared altogether, and he was tempted to keep on to the real island, the one almost two miles away with the chateau at its crest. Anne had promised they'd picnic there one day, but she never had found the time since, she'd said, when they did go they must not have to rush back for anything. They must plan it carefully that way. But soon the tide would begin to rise again, so, feeling out of sorts and bored, he sauntered back to the house just as Anne and Raoul and Suzanne came driving down the lane.

They were unnaturally silent as they got out of the car, Suzanne looking up at her mother worriedly, holding fast to her hand.

"There is a letter for you," said Anne coldly, to Julian. "I have one also. It will say that your mother is coming to St. Pierre-de-la-Mer to stay for a few days rather than let you go back to Paris alone." Then, unsmiling, she went into her house.

It was with a sense of shock that Julian read that his mother would be there in three days to take him home.

"Don't let Mme Devereux see this," the letter cautioned. "But do you think she will invite me to stay with you until we are ready to leave? I should think she might—I would in her place—but if you think she will not, then do make reservations for me at some inn, if there is a decent one nearby. Or if there isn't—after all, I have to stay some place, at least overnight."

What was he supposed to do? Anyhow, Anne solved it herself, saying the Hotel Marc in the village was the place where most English people stayed; she would call them at once and see that they reserved a room with bath for Mrs. Hadley.

"Your mother, is she pretty?" asked Anne that night, a strangely plaintive note in her voice. "Is she chic and very

rich, Julian? Does she wear very, very beautiful clothes?"
she went on relentlessly, for anyone could see this embarrassed him. And what could he answer?

"Just ordinary, I guess," he said. She certainly wasn't
rich, he knew, and he said that, but Anne spoke crossly to
Raoul.

"Now, my friend, you will have a beautiful American
woman to admire, to show you how poor and ugly I am."
Then she jumped up from the table, saying, "Come, Suzanne! Why you do not come?"

Confusedly Julian got to his feet when Raoul did. "My
mother isn't—isn't beautiful like you, Anne," he said, some
instinct to reassure her hurrying him on, yet he was more
surprised than ever when she turned and threw her arms
about his neck, kissing his cheek.

"Ah, *mon ami!*" she cried, then held him off, herself
again, laughing. "I did not know how salty a boy's skin can
be!" For an instant she stopped being foolish or nervous
and looked so tender and loving Julian felt his heart would
burst. He wanted to tell her then that he didn't have to
leave her, that he didn't want to, ever, some crazy thing
like that—but Raoul was staring at them, all teasing gone
from his face.

"You are the *bébé*, Anne," he said, a tight sadness which
Julian had not seen before appearing at the corners of his
mouth. "More young, I think, than Julian here, and much
more foolish, *ma chérie.*"

"But I am young, like Julian!" she cried, animation
bringing an unexpected flush to her thin cheeks. "I have
sixteen years, and I am virgin!"

Julian had never seen anyone so funny or so wonderful,
and as they sat down again at the table Raoul jumped up
and brought back the bottle of Calvados, pouring out a
glass for each of them (not so much for Julian but more

than he'd had before). Anne, lifting hers, began singing one of Suzanne's songs about a little prince who offers a girl his hand which Julian had heard, but with Raoul beating time with his fork it seemed to have new meaning.

"*Quand je dis parti, le petit prince a dit—*" And then Anne looked at Raoul. "I forget," she said quietly. "I do not know all the words."

"The little prince, he promise to return," he said and they were both quiet, looking at each other. "The song says '*Lundi, Mardi, Mercredi, Jeudi, Vendredi—*'"

"*Mais non pas Dimanche,* that is too late. On Sunday the little prince, he is tired of coming back!"

Raoul did not offer to carry Suzanne upstairs that night and Anne left them alone at the table, disappearing into the upper silence with the child. Raoul smoked one cigarette after another, and finally offered one to Julian, who took it, grateful for this gesture to his maturity.

"We do not tell Anne," said Raoul. "But all boys break rules sometimes. And you are not quite a boy, I think, Julian. . . . Do you think she is very beautiful, our Anne?" he asked quietly.

"Oh, sure," said Julian, and of course at that moment his voice had to crack. "I guess anybody would say that," he added, getting it back in control. So then he could ask what he'd wanted to know for a long time. "Did you know Maurice Devereux, Raoul? I mean, were you a friend of his in the war or something?"

Raoul inhaled deeply before he answered, and then exhaled. "No, I am afraid not. I was in a German prison camp those years. Maurice was left behind—he was the great hero of the Résistance, you know. There is a fine bronze plaque on the wall near Notre Dame where he was shot."

"I know." Julian hesitated, struck by that about the

prison camp. Maybe he should feel sorry for Raoul, too, except that he was here, and alive.

"He was a—what you say, a great guy," added the Frenchman.

"I should *think* so," said Julian, forgetting to smoke his cigarette. "I guess nobody ever gets over knowing somebody like that, somebody so brave, I mean. I guess *she'll* never get over it."

"Perhaps that is true."

Raoul carefully tapped his ashes in a blue saucer. "So—your mother, she come soon. And then you go back to America. What will you tell your friends, Julian? How patriotic we are in *la belle France?* How we never forget our dead, how we have not the good sense to leave all that? You have heroes in America, also—but I think it is not so—not the same."

Julian somehow understood Raoul was upset by the way he crushed his cigarette in the saucer, although he could not guess why at the moment. But the Frenchman smoked too much, his mother would say, and he was never still; and tonight he looked younger and not confident about anything.

"We have heroes, sure," Julian said, thinking his way through an answer. "I guess it isn't the same thing, though. Like Lincoln, and George Washington—and we don't think much about them except on their birthdays." He spoke regretfully, even apologetically, but Raoul surprisingly didn't seem to understand this.

"Exactly." The Frenchman's handsome face was unnaturally stern. "I understand, and that is good. No ghosts for Americans, no shadows in the present. . . . Will you tell your friends for me, for Raoul, that you are lucky?" He had lighted a fresh cigarette, but now stubbed it out in the dish filled to overflowing with butts. "Well, *bonne nuit*, Julian. *Dormez bien!*"

"*Bon soir*, Raoul," returned the boy, wishing they could talk longer, having at last found something interesting to talk about. But Raoul bounded up the stairs two at a time, and Julian followed to his own room, when it seemed the house became unnaturally silent almost at once, as though everyone in it badly needed rest.

It was odd how nervous Anne became before his mother's arrival. She spoke French almost entirely, and scolded Suzanne in a shrill, unnatural voice. She even seemed to make quarrels with Raoul, and ignored Julian. Then one day she accused everyone of forgetting Maurice Devereux. "One has obligations to the dead," she reproached them. "We must not forget what France owes to its great heroes!"

Julian said quickly, "But I go to the grave every day, Anne. Almost—"

She stared at him, the slow color spreading from her neck across her pale golden cheeks and forehead.

"An American boy—and you do this!" Then she burst into tears.

Julian felt confused, but at dinner that night she was all right again and came down smiling in a flame-colored blouse they hadn't seen before and the gold earrings. After they'd finished the first bottle of *cidre* she insisted they open another, and they were gayer than ever they had been. She laughed at Raoul and teased Julian so that when they got up from the table he couldn't help it, he caught her suddenly and impulsively about the waist and swung her around and around.

For an instant she clung to him, laughing, but when he could not seem to let go her mood changed and she demanded to be freed. Suzanne ran around them crying,

"Non, non, non, Julian!" But there was a hard core of wilfulness in him that would not let go, like a hold one got in wrestling sometimes when you couldn't release your opponent. Instead of freeing her he held her tighter, his face hot and excitement mounting like a wild thing in his breast until Raoul came over and roughly jerked him away.

"Be careful, young American bull! A woman is not strong and tough like you!"

Shocked with self-blame Julian stood before them breathing heavily, hating Raoul with all his heart. He did not quite dare to look at Anne before he turned and ran out of the house into the dark sea-smelling night. Not stopping until he reached the rocks, he climbed down to a ledge near the octopus holes now exposed halfway to the sea, where he watched the tide rising in the moonlight and did not move until the water almost touched the soles of his feet. When he had to scramble back to dryness his foot slipped, kicking off a loose rock and he would have fallen, plummeting into the sea if he'd not just managed to catch hold of a tree limb higher than his head and pull himself to safety.

For a long time he lay on the high rock shelf until he heard Anne's voice, reedlike and frightened, calling, "Julian, Julian! *Chéri*—where are you?"

And even though he wanted not to answer he could not stop himself from getting up and going to her where she stood anxiously waiting in the lighted doorway, a silhouette which stirred his heart with a dark and painful love.

His mother came next afternoon. Julian was on the beach tossing the red ball to the French girl, Minette, when Raoul came to say she had arrived.

He found Anne and his mother sitting stiffly in the parlor which was seldom used, and as he bent over to kiss her he sensed her nervousness. She was almost a stranger in her tan city suit, and she looked at him as though she did not remember him very well, either.

"How brown you are," she kept saying. "And you have grown. I know Julian has grown inches," she insisted, further embarrassing him, as Anne never would. Anne sat smiling like a diffident schoolgirl, but it flashed into Julian's mind that there wasn't as much difference in their ages as he had thought, and some of the fellows at school had even said his mother was a "good looking dame"; she always looked about the same to him.

Anne excused herself, saying she must go look after Suzanne, and forgot to invite his mother to stay for lunch.

"She's a beautiful woman," his mother said as they walked down the road to the inn, "but is she always so unfriendly?"

"She's not unfriendly," Julian protested, but then he saw his mother might think so judging Anne by the way she was today. "She's sure been nice to me," he said, defensively.

Glancing at him with an appraising smile, his mother made another of those remarks he hated. "You're not a little boy any longer," she said. "I must say, though, I did think Mme Devereux would ask me for lunch this first day."

"Anne never thinks of things like that," he said, wishing this were so. "Besides, we've got a pretty full house with Raoul there."

"Oh, yes, M. Poignant." His mother looked thoughtful and somewhat amused. "Well, as I said before, Mme Devereux is a very beautiful woman—"

He had lunch with her at the inn, which was one he'd seen in the distance from the beach, and they talked about letters from his father, and going home, things like that until his mother yawned and said she guessed maybe she'd take a nap that afternoon, if he didn't mind. She'd had some pretty late nights with friends in Paris and this salt

air made her sleepy. Why didn't he bring his friends back
to the hotel for a drink around five?

Released, Julian ran back up-hill to the lane leading to
the yellow house, with a sense of panic that they might have
gone off somewhere without him. But Anne and Raoul and
Suzanne were still at the table as he noisily drew back the
chair at his usual place.

"My mother would like for you to come for cocktails,"
he announced. "And bring Suzanne. I'll look after her."
Now surely they would see that his mother didn't want to
to be left out of things.

Anne looked obliquely at Raoul and said something so
fast Julian could not catch it. The Frenchman returned her
look with a grin, then closed his eyes lazily, slowly uncross-
ing his long legs, and leaning back to stretch. Then he
shrugged. It was the kind of look no one could comprehend
unless one had been born among them, but Julian could
understand that Raoul was laughing at Anne.

She tossed her head and sat up very straight and tall.

"But this is the day we have a *picnique* on the island,"
she said. "That makes the difficulty."

Julian asked eagerly, "The island? Can I come with you?"

Anne looked as though she would refuse, then the
warmth and natural laughter came back. "These spoiled
Americans," she chided. "Always they must miss nothing.
Yes, Julian, you will come with us because you must not say
the Frenchwoman, she does not know how to spoil men also.
We will have a *picnique*. Just as we say, we will take you to
the island today! Suzanne will stay with Catharine."

Overcome with happiness, Julian ran to get his bathing
trunks and then they were down at the water's edge and
getting in the motor boat of a neighbor who was going
fishing and said he would take them across. There was no
time to tell his mother, for the tide would soon change;

perhaps in a few hours it would be low enough to wade back in time for cocktails at the hotel after all, Anne said.

When they reached the big island in the Channel with the farm and chateau on top, the tide had already turned and the biggest rocks were beginning to rise exposed like sentinels from the sea.

For a time the three of them explored the shores of the island after the fisherman left them in his boat. Anne walked ahead in her bright flowered skirt and yellow blouse, the wind lifting the soft wisps of hair from her slender neck and the sun bringing out the gold in her skin. She led them to a cove where she said Julian might catch fish with lines they had brought and then sat with him awhile as Raoul went climbing up the center of the island to see the farm. Julian was wondering if he'd get a bite when the fish began going after his bait and he brought in a big one, then a smaller one, and once Anne got up and hugged him because he was having such good luck. He did not want to be rude, but when she left him at last in answer to a call from Raoul —the farm was abandoned, he'd yelled, but he wanted to show Anne something—Julian was relieved. He did not want to lose one minute of the sport, for never had he seen fish bite that way before.

He did not know how long he had been at it when he noticed that the tide which he thought was still going out, had begun to rise noticeably, and he was surprised to see that it was getting late. Anne had said she might take a nap behind the rocks and maybe she'd forgotten what time they'd planned on starting back. Still he hoped she'd give him just a little while longer until he caught a few more big ones. His mother would understand if they were too late for her cocktails; they could all have dinner at the hotel instead.

When he thought again about his surroundings he was

startled to see the last rock in the distance suddenly sink under the rising tide. Uneasily he stood looking back over the island wondering where Anne and Raoul had gone. "Anne," he called once, but there was not even an echo to his voice.

For a while he skirted the shore of the island, and the octopus rocks in the distance seemed almost as far away as England. It was then he got scared. The breeze was stronger, a few clouds were gathering, and nobody seemed to be anywhere at all. Even the few small fishing boats seemed to be moving faster off on the horizon.

He yelled their names, walking hurriedly and wondering if the neighbor's boat could have come back and picked them up. He'd been so intent on his fishing that maybe they'd called him, and then decided he'd walked back at low tide, alone. Or maybe he'd misunderstood, the way one did, sometimes, with their English or his French. A part of his mind was getting hard to control, and he was taking a deep breath to let out a really big holler when he saw the edge of Anne's flowered skirt sticking out from behind some rocks. He could have died with relief, knowing that Raoul must be there also.

He had begun scrambling down over the rocks when the skirt was drawn back suddenly and Anne's foot moved oddly in the shadows of the rocks and he heard the sound of muffled laughter. Then again there was silence; but he did not expect to find them as they were when he moved far enough to see them lying under the ledge of rock together. Anne was half-sitting, half-lying back in a hollow, careless as a girl in her pose, and Raoul was bent over her, gently nuzzling her breasts as she stroked the back of his head. There was a silent moment of embrace during which Julian could not breathe; then Anne sat up.

"*Mon Dieu!*" she cried at once. "Raoul, *regardes!* We are trapped by the tide!"

Raoul did not even look; instead he laughed and caught hold of her hands, pulling her down again. And for another instant—

They must have heard Julian as he turned and scrambled away back up the rocks kicking some loose stones down on them, but he did not care.

"Julian!" Anne called, and he had to turn back seeing her trying to straighten her blouse and her hair. Then she looked again at the horizon, as Raoul was doing, and they began talking very fast together as though the disappearing rocks, the rising water, and the elongating distance between them and the mainland had really taken them by surprise. But Julian kept walking rapidly to the small sandy cove where they'd landed and left their lunch a long, long time ago, feeling no comfort at all in having found them.

It was after ten that night before the tide dropped low enough for them to think of wading back. The boat hadn't come, and they had eaten their picnic lunch, with Anne and Raoul making jokes, pretending they were neither worried nor embarrassed; but Julian felt a deep, resentful shame for them both. He was no baby not to understand what had been going on back there: hadn't he and Jacques and Michel seen the same thing in that tent on the beach? Now he understood why he had never liked Raoul, even from the start. Let him talk and laugh, pretending they were friends. . . . And what about his mother waiting at the hotel for them to come to her party?

Yet a sorrow kept catching at his heart, subduing it. The enormity of Anne's deceit went deep inside him, thinking first of all that she was the wife of a hero, wasn't she? of Maurice, his friend. She was unworthy, no better than one

of the *petites filles* Michel and Jacques had boasted they
would have in bed themselves before long. . . . He could not
draw away fast enough when she put her cold hand on his
arm.

She looked at him strangely. "You are cold, Julian. You
will be sick—and Raoul, they will say it is my fault! If you
have not permitted me to sleep back there," she scolded, as
though there had been no more to it than that. "Raoul, you
should have been stern, you should have made me wake! My
baby, she will be crying, too, for her mama!"

Julian could not help saying, "Good thing she didn't
come along." But they were too stupid to see he meant this
more ways than one, or to care that his teeth were chattering because he felt cold and miserable and hurt inside.

Raoul said, "I have notice the rising tide, but it is too late
then, to wade back. So, I permit you to sleep. Now we have
only to wait."

By the time the tide was noticeably lower the bright
moon hung like a lantern in the sky to throw a path of
light from their feet to the mainland. Now it was time to
go, Raoul said, walking up to the edge of the sea and stepping in. Anne followed and then Julian, the black water
frightening and cold and repellent as a grave, and the tide
tugged and pulled on their legs and bodies as though to
draw them further out to sea; but at least it was not too
deep to make a few steps of progress toward the mainland.

They kept close together, testing their footings but feeling strange and heavy-burdened in their shoes, which Raoul
said they must not remove. The moon was rising so that each
figure waded in his own separate path of light, but so per-
ishable that the brief passing of a cloud could leave them
stranded in the darkness. Further out the water rose above
their waists and then to their armpits, but it got no deeper
after that, and the moon remained free. Then it was the tide

they minded, relentless as a heavy wind and pulling them back, so that Raoul said they could see how dangerous it would be if they tried to swim. Once, when a sudden flowering of phosphorescence burst around them he pointed out how fast the tide moved it from their path.

At first Anne kept talking, exclaiming, even shouting now and then toward the shore in brave good humor. Bravely, Julian had to admit; she sounded braver than he felt. Raoul kept just ahead of them, cautioning them to stay close in his wake.

"Walk carefully, Julian. Do not lift your feet high but slide along the bottom. Watch out for sudden holes. We are safe if we hold to a steady path, together."

They talked as though their own voices could protect them against the danger, and at least it passed the time. So when they paused to look back they could exclaim how they had made more progress than they had thought.

Raoul slipped once under water and for an instant Anne's voice ceased, her hand slapped hard against her mouth. But before anyone could move to help Raoul he was on his feet again, laughing at himself.

"The Champs Élysées was never like this," he exclaimed, in boyish bravado. The next moment Anne slipped and would have gone under, too, if Raoul and Julian had not caught her at the same instant. Even so, her head was submerged in the black sea; when they started on again, she did not talk or laugh until they reached the first rock where they stopped to rest. Julian thought then she was crying, and this so unnerved him that he could not, at the moment, find the anger he was nursing for her.

"Your mother will be angry, no?" she asked, as they huddled close together on a dark slippery rock, and then she reached out to touch his wet hair as though to brush it back from his forehead.

"She probably will be," he agreed, coldly, drawing away.

"It is my fault, all my fault," she moaned, hugging her thin body like a mermaid shivering in the moonlight. "Why do we stay so long, Raoul? Let us go on. Let us go quickly!" and she slid down ahead of them with a splash into the water.

Julian did not want to admire or to pity her just then. You know it *is* your fault, he thought accusingly; but when Raoul said it would be better if they held hands so perhaps they could make way more continuously, Julian felt a pain of compassion as her wet narrow palm pressed against his.

The black immensity of the sea did not diminish, although the darkness was not as terrifying as at first, until Julian felt some deep-sea creature brush past his leg. His heart in his mouth, he jerked away; and once to their left, there was a disturbance as though some powerful animal resented being aroused. This subsided also, but Raoul had looked apprehensively at the spot where it had been.

"What was that?" cried Anne, putting her long white hand to her throat and stopping as though to turn back.

"*Rien!*" said Raoul, but moving them on rather more quickly through the water.

Ahead on the mainland they could see flashlights now on the point jutting out beyond the clearing where Maurice Devereux was buried. As it was the nearest point to the islands, it seemed that they had been missed and perhaps an alarm sounded: Being marooned was not the ordinary thing Anne and Raoul tried to make it seem, Julian understood now, but the kind of accident anyone who knew the water and the tides must learn to dread. Once Julian thought he heard his mother's voice calling above the others; it was at that moment the disturbance in the water came again.

Unaccountably, fear struck like the return of a boomerang at what might be closing in on them from the sides and from the rear. Under this black sucking water who could say what might be lurking at every step to catch a foot or leg or draw them down in quicksand to its depth? Giant crabs, sharks and octopi, all the sea life glimpsed under a daylight sky magnified a thousand times by night—and for an instant Julian was afraid even of putting his next foot down! Then Anne cried out that something had brushed her leg.

"*J'ai peur,*" she whispered, her voice seeming to carry a long way through the night. "*J'ai peur—*" And they both drew closer to her.

Julian's own fear seemed less as she clung to him, and he even pointed out how fast the tide was receding, how near they were to shore and the figures they could now make out waiting on the rocks above. Lights were being flashed upon the water, and upon the strange looking insects they themselves must seem here on the black sullen face of the sea. The three of them splashing more than ever, as though to frighten away whatever might be near, and the water rose in a blinding spray before their eyes—still they tried to hurry, to move faster toward the shore.

Then, as though the floor of the sea had been pulled from under him, Raoul fell from sight, snatching his hand from Anne's as he did so, to vanish beneath the surface. Anne cried out, "Raoul!" as though bereaved, and Julian, almost without thought, plunged ahead until he, too, fell sharply down where the floor of the channel seemed to have dropped away into bottomless space. It was one of those holes Raoul had warned them might appear without warning, but lulled by their proximity to the shore even he had gotten careless. Raoul came up as Julian also was sucked down by the current, and they caught each other—but it was Julian who pulled Raoul to the surface, their feet on sandy bottom at last but thrust back some ten feet from where Raoul had gone down.

Anne wisely had not moved, so, cautiously, they changed their course to reach her, Raoul insisting still on leading the way; and finally they climbed on the last rock but one to rest before making the final crossing to the shore.

They remained longer than usual there, Raoul breathing very hard and Anne crouched against him, her head resting on his knee.

"You saved my life," said Raoul as Julian looked away. "I was not prepared—for a moment I think, I cannot save myself! And there you were, my friend!"

"Lucky for us you went down first," said Julian, trying to speak carelessly. "It's a good thing, too, you didn't have to pull Anne and me out at the same time."

"I could not have helped," said Anne sadly. "I am too weak, I am only a woman who cannot save herself."

Raoul looked down on her head, dark with wet and the shadows made by the moonlight, and Julian watched both of them.

"It is true, Anne," Raoul said quietly. "You are only a woman. . . . Perhaps you are not so strong as you believe." Then he patted her shoulder as though he had made a joke. "I think you need a man all the time, to look after you. Why do you not marry Julian—or me?"

Anne sat up pushing the hair back from her temples with the palms of both hands. "This time, I think we come to the shore," she said, with a hint of laughter in her voice. Then resolutely she stepped once more into the water.

"You will have a story for your friends, I think, Julian," said Raoul as they went in after her. "I think after this they will call you Moby Dick."

"They wouldn't believe a thing like this," said Julian, but considering how he would tell them, just the same.

"How can one believe what one has not known?" asked Anne. "But—you must tell them, Julian. Say, one may be caught in tides one does not make!"

"Tides change," said Raoul in a voice curiously edged with anger. "As one sees: one waits a little, one plumbs the depths, one takes one's courage in one's hand. *Et, voilà!* That is destiny! Is it not true, Julian?"

"I think so," he said, not understanding but examining the unexpectedly warm feeling of friendship which had come over him. And almost the next instant they found themselves on sand which brought them to knee depth, their bodies rising clear of the sea, safe, alive. When at last they climbed up over the rocks into the full circle of light, the villagers came and gathered around them as though they were rescued sailors from a storm—as in a sense they were. Everyone chattered and asked questions, and explained how there had been a misunderstanding; it seemed the neighbor who had taken them to the island in his boat had not understood they would not return before high tide. Now he had gone on a roundabout way to the island to bring them back; if they had waited there all would have been well.

Julian felt a warm touch of a hand on his cold arm and there was Minette, who thrust a roll of crusty bread into his hands. Her grandmother stood watching, it seemed with approval, as he thanked the girl, and then they both stood back when his mother, wrapped in her big tan coat, hurried up with a hotel blanket over her arm. She had been crying and Anne paused to explain, until Raoul urgently drew her on, telling her she must put on dry clothes and take no more risks.

"Julian, my poor darling," his mother was crying, "you must have been so frightened, out there in that black freezing water, caught in that awful tide!" She was trying to hold the musty-smelling blanket around his cold but proud shoulders; she would not stop talking. "And sharks, some-one saw a shark out there just this afternoon! Close to shore!—Oh, if your father hears of this, I don't know what he'll say. No one told me how dangerous it could be!"

"Let's get going, please," he said, his teeth chattering. "I'm okay now. Lay off, can't you, Ma?"

She stared at him for one reproachful moment as Minette passed again—in the light from a parked car he saw her eyes filled with tender sympathy—and he felt enraged with the whole world of adults. At least someone his age would *know* how he felt.

Raoul had the bottle of Calvados and four glasses on the table when they reached the house. Anne was coming downstairs with Suzanne wrapped in a blanket in her arms, her own skirt still wet, although she'd changed her blouse for a sweater and put on her big floppy house slippers. Raoul began to scold her, and then put his own dry towel around her on top of the sweater, his arm clinging to her shoulder in a way Julian knew his mother noticed by the way her eyes suddenly became sharp and wise.

"Papa Raoul," said Suzanne, holding her arms out for him and at the same time giving Julian a sleepy smile.

"Now," said Raoul, holding the child in one arm and al-most gaily pouring the little glasses quite full. "A toast for our hero, Julian. A fine fisherman—whose fish all got away!"

The fish! Not until this moment had Julian thought of what he'd left behind.

"A very little one for me," said his mother, then gasped as she saw Julian take a glass from the tray. "Good heavens, Julian doesn't drink that!" Then she asked in a smaller voice, as his gangling height seemed to tower over her. "Or does he?"

"I like it," said Julian. This was of course not quite true, and Raoul's amused eyes could have told her so, but Mildred felt too defeated, too left out of things now to be sure of anything she saw. Solemnly they raised their glasses, clinking them, and Raoul said: "To life!"

To life. Raoul's eyes met Julian's as though this toast was something he would understand, and as though he wanted Julian to see what it was. Why?

Because I know, thought Julian. Because we both know that Maurice Devereux is forgotten now by Anne: by everyone. Because he's dead, and we're alive!

Suddenly he put down his glass, knowing what he had to do. Raoul looked out of the corners of his long clear eyes, although he kept on talking to the women and did not stop when Julian, mumbling he'd be back in a minute, left the room.

"Now where has he gone?" he heard his mother ask as he ran through the kitchen to the back entrance. She sounded worried, but said no more after a quiet answer from Raoul.

Overhead the sky was black and formless, and the smell of rain was on the air. A strong wind had risen and by the time Julian reached the mound leaves were darting wildly from the wooded path near the lane, while off below he could see the white caps of the waves whipped to fever froth by the sudden gale. In a little while it will be raining, he thought. What if we were out there in that water then?

For a moment he dwelled on what they had gone through, and perhaps had missed. Sharks, and quicksand, ledges, storm—They'd come through it all, safe and sound; he had even saved Raoul's life!

With a start he became aware that he had been standing by the grave of Maurice Devereux for some time, yet all there was in his mind was his own adventure, his own heroism. Where was the apology he had come to make, what was his own bravery worth compared with the heroism of Maurice Devereux?

He threw himself down on the grassy mound close to the wooden cross and tried to recapture the feeling he'd once had for the great dead man. He thought how the Frenchman had stood before a firing squad without even a cover for his eyes, laughing, daring them to shoot—and for one brief flash he did recapture something, some memory of the hero, of Maurice, his friend. For a moment he even thought, How terrible not to be alive, *How awful to be dead when everyone else is alive.*

But was this what he had felt before? Pity, and regret? In confusion Julian tried to remember—and knew that it was not. He had not, actually, felt that Maurice Devereux was dead but more vital and more present than anyone he knew. That it was they, the living, who were not quite real—

A gust of wind brought his thin cotton shirt flapping from his belt and Julian shivered. Out over the rocks the waves were splashing audibly, and further beyond was the steady lonesome roar of the sea. In the village below there were still a few lights, one, he thought, in the cottage of Minette and her grandmother. Then that, too, was extinguished. The world seemed very dark.

There's not much use staying out here any longer, he thought, somehow apologizing to the still, small, shadowy mound. I can't do any good here now, and it's cold. I'd better be getting back—

Back at the house it seemed they'd offered his mother the guest room and she was going to stay.

"Otherwise, you would have to take her to the hotel," said Anne, leading his mother up the stairs, and for a mo-

ment both women smiled down at him from the landing.
They liked each other, after all.

Raoul held Suzanne asleep on his shoulder as he began to
close the windows against the rain which had just begun. In
a moment it was coming down in earnest, bringing the fragrance of honeysuckle and wet pine into the room. Julian
helped him put the last window down.

"We will be sorry to lose you, Julian," said Raoul, and
Suzanne's dark head stirred under his chin, but she did not
awaken. "You have made much good for Anne, Julian. Do
you know that? I think you have brought her from the past
as I could not do," he added quietly.

"I have?" For an instant Julian wondered if Raoul was
pulling his leg, but the handsome Frenchman seemed very
serious.

"Yes, I think she will marry me, now."

It sounded so natural the way he said this that Julian
wasn't even surprised; it was only in the next instant he
thought of other things, Maurice again, and Suzanne—

"Suzanne and I," Raoul continued in his oddly insistent
way, and almost as though he had read Julian's thoughts,
"have much for which to thank you."

"I don't think I did anything," said Julian, as the child,
beginning to awaken, thrust one soft, curling hand back
over Raoul's arm. "She's going to be a beauty someday," he
said, at random.

"Like her mother, fortunately," Raoul said humorously.
"Not like me."

Startled, Julian met the smiling dark eyes in the Frenchman's face as the child stirred, passing her small fist over
heavy lids, then opening her own dark eyes wide and clear.
The color and even the shape, Julian saw, were the same—

"So that's the way it is," said Raoul, in a general way.
"Now shall we catch up on our sleep? You will have dreams

tonight, I am sure. If you feel a shark biting your leg, just yell, and I will come to save you!"

But Julian did not dream of sharks. Instead his dreams were surprisingly pleasant, like the taste of the good bread Minette had thrust into his hands when they came up out of the dark sea. And then it seemed he and the French girl were chasing each other on the beach in some sort of game until, for one breathless moment, they evaded the sharp eyes of her grandmother behind the big black rocks and kissed until Minette broke away and threw him her red ball. They tossed this rapidly back and forth, back and forth, back and forth at a crazy speed until suddenly it flew off like a shot into the air. Then again he was running after Minette, catching her this time on a mound of sand into which they sank until some of it got in his nose and made him sneeze. . . .

He woke up sneezing, with Catharine calling from downstairs that someone was there to see him. Dressing hurriedly, he ran down to find Minette standing tall in the bright sunlight of the open door. The rain had come and gone in the night, and the green leaves behind her were washed clean and shining as she waited for him in her yellow dress, the big red ball, recaptured, in her arms.

Heart Is a
Masculine Noun

The American woman and the little boy could be seen every noon and evening walking from the Hotel Beaupére along the rue Madame toward the Pension du Coeur where they took their meals. Alexis got so he timed his departure from his own small room by the moment of their stepping out upon the street, although he watched until they entered the gate at No. 22 on the rue Madame before leaving his window. The woman had a young, graceful walk, a dark, shining crown of hair, and a beautiful face already tanned (unlike a Parisian's) by the summer sun.

The child, unexceptional in any way, had thin, long legs, bristling red hair generally in disorder, and the attitude of a leashed terrier quivering to meet every challenge. Yet he aroused no feeling of like or dislike in Alexis until it became evident how jealously the boy made demands upon the mother. He could not bear for her to pause and speak to anyone without pulling irritably on her arm, and it seemed odd that the woman remained undisturbed by the boy's possessiveness, smiling on him frequently and tenderly as if she thought he were an angel by her side.

"The boy is not a nice boy," Alexis said in English each day at his washstand mirror. (Some years ago his American teacher had advised this form of practice.) And sweeping the silver-crested brushes back over his thinning hair, he pronounced: "The American boy is a rude boy!" but added thoughtfully, "Yet the woman—she is so lovely!"

The first time when he turned away from his own attentive image, it occurred to him that a revelation of some importance had taken place. This may have been because, although he had long admired America and hoped some day to go there, he had never before quite believed in the reality of an American woman's beauty. But by the fourth day the sight of her began to stir his imagination as would a photograph found in the attic of his youth. This was a paradox: that a woman from the new world should revive nostalgia for the old.

Looking into his mirror that noon Alexis practiced more ardently than usual, "*She* is lovely. She *is* lovely. She is love-*ly!*" dragging out the last syllable, his expression soft enough to melt a stone.

Away from his room, however, he felt slightly foolish about the whole thing. "Why," he asked himself cynically, running nimbly enough for his fifty years down the four flights of stairs, "should this thing happen to you, Alexis Alexandrovitch Gronsky, at such a moment of your life? Are you crazy perhaps? Or ill?"

He even sought an answer from his old friend Guido, who worked at the movie studios at Billancourt and had often advised him to cultivate American women who came alone to Paris. "Why is such a woman here with only a child?" he asked Guido. "Has she no husband to keep her home? Surely only a fool of a man would trust such beauty away from his care—unless she is cold! She has no love for any man, perhaps?"

"American women are always hungry for romance," Guido solemnly asserted, having been to America three times. "That is why they so often come to Europe alone. It is the husbands who have no romance in their souls, who are cold!"

"But the child? How can she expect romance with a child at her side?"

Guido threw up his hands. "And when did having a child ever prevent any woman from making love, my friend?"

"That is true!" cried Alexis, suddenly recalling certain episodes from his own past. "Doors can be locked against them!"

"You see? So speak to her, Alexis, have no fear. She is no doubt longing equally for a sign from you!"

He could have told Guido, of course, that this was impossible, for although he had watched the woman every day, only once could she have seen him when they chanced to pass on the hotel stairs. Even then he had not spoken to her, having his pride in exile as in his own country before the Communists took over. He could not approach a stranger as easily as that.

Yet he would find a way if he could make up his mind about three things: first, that the American was truly in need of love; two, that she would understand his own virtues if he were bold enough to approach her; and three, most important of all, that she would be kind.

It was on the sixth day that Alexis came to his conclusions: that a woman who moved with such sensuous grace and rhythm must surely suffer torments without a lover; that such beauty could not exist without womanly understanding; and finally, since she was kind even to that dreadful child, she could not be cruel to any man.

So, convinced of these elemental truths, on the seventh day of his infatuation, Alexis decided to return to the Pension du Coeur.

Alexis saw that in twenty years much had changed at the pension of Mme and Mlle du Coeur. When Alexis had dined there before, immediately following World War II, Americans were too rich and important to stay anywhere but at the Crillon or the Ritz or the George V, and only other exiles like himself had sought out these unpretentious pensions on the Left Bank. But such banding together was only a continuation of exile—exile being that monogamy of the mind with which one accepts but one country, one love for a lifetime—and so he had separated himself from the inward-turning, reminiscing eyes of the others and had found work with the Americans in their vast and complex organization. After this, he had felt justified in moving to the tourist-patronized hotel, which had seemed to him to be more the American way of life; he had also dined where they dined (if it was not *trop cher*); listened constantly to their speech; and dreamed that eventually all this might lead him across the seas where he would then, even more dramatically, forget the old life in the new. But years had passed, and still he was in Paris.

Now, the irony was that American children were dominating the Pension du Coeur, running up and down the stairs, snatching their American cameras hanging from the hall rack, their voices and all the other echoes of both English and American sounds creating the atmosphere of an afternoon at a zoo.

"*Mais certainment*," Madame du Coeur assured him as he bent respectfully over her white and withered hand. "There will always be a place for Count Gronsky at the Pension du Coeur." It did not matter that her faded blue eyes mocked

him with the disbelief of the old for the dreams of the un-
defeated—although for a proud moment Alexis' eyes turned
from hers, seeing only by accident the wooden plaque hanging over her head. Some American child had carved and sent
this back, long before the War, as a gift:

> *L'amour, l'amour*
> *To the Pension de la Coeur.*

It had always amused everyone, he recalled, that the child
had thought "heart" was a feminine noun.

On the eighth day Alexis watched for the departure of
the woman before he stepped briskly from the tiny hotel
elevator, and out upon the street at a discreet distance behind her and the red-haired child. It was a mild, pleasant
day, and there seemed to be smiles on the faces of nearly
everyone, a spring to every step.

Alexis raced up the winding stairs like a schoolboy, finding the pension buzzing with talk as he came in the door,
and all the faces he saw looked friendly and kind. The
woman had vanished, but he could wait; and then to his dismay he was sent into the anteroom among the students and
new patrons who had not yet proved themselves worthy of
the larger room where Madame and Mademoiselle Jacqueline presided at their separate tables, where there were the
English tea service, the paintings, and the great chest of
Madame's distinguished ancestors. *There* was acceptance
while *here* was only another form of exile.

It was a long, rather frustrating week before anything
happened. Alexis watched the American woman on the
street, saw her disappear into the room among her chattering countrymen, and once was within striking distance of
the child whom he believed dominated the mother with
utter selfishness. After six days shut out of the salon with

the privileged ones, Alexis almost decided to return no
more, and so he left ten minutes late from the hotel one
noon to show his displeasure. Better the old Madame's anger,
he thought, than the neglect of all the world.

Yet he was no longer so foolishly brave as in his youth,
and at the last minute hurried up the stairs in order to be on
time for the entrée. Breathless when he reached the landing,
it was then he came upon the American woman standing at
the door as though she were waiting for him.

Alexis's delight almost made him do an unwise thing, to
speak as though they had been introduced. Then he recalled
in time that she could not even know his name as he now
knew hers—Mrs. Andrews—so he stepped back, with a
slight bow, his eyes averted until she said in a warm, low
voice, "Since we are both late, perhaps Madame will only be
half as angry with each of us!"

Alexis was so delighted that he bowed low in the manner
of his youth, flashing great dark eyes and smiling so broadly
the waxed ends of his mustache pricked his sallow cheeks.

"Even the old one could not be angry with a lady so
charming as you, Madame Andrews!"

She looked briefly startled by his ardor, but then she
smiled enchantingly, her blue eyes limpid as an Irish girl's,
her teeth small and white and even. "But a Frenchwoman
forgives a man more quickly than a woman, Count Gronsky!"

Alexis was so amazed that she knew his name that he did
not even notice how Mademoiselle's eyes brightened signifi-
cantly when they stepped into the narrow hallway where
she was standing. It was only when Mlle Jacqueline finally
invited him into the larger room that he understood that
now nothing was unattainable.

The Americans knew each other well and the table was

extravagant with their laughter and plans and conversation. Yet they listened respectfully when Alexis spoke—often enough, he hoped, to show how well he knew their language. And when the eyes of other women sought him out, he hoped Mrs. Andrews noticed this, but understood that his own looks were only for her.

If she did not, however, her child did; as early as the second day Alexis surprised a disconcertingly antagonistic look from the boy directed exclusively against himself, which he returned coldly. By the third day it came to him that he disliked this boy, Robin, more than any child he had ever known; and, protest though he would, insist as though the mother herself had intercepted this thought, Alexis was forced to admit the awful truth that the boy was a monster, even though the other guests patted him on the head and conversed with him as though he were quite normal. And when the mother spoke to Alexis, her large blue eyes sometimes shadowed from her surely sleepless, lonely nights, thus stirring Alexis to the depths, the boy clamored for her attention.

"Come on, let's go," he was forever whining, having bolted his food like a barbarian. Meeting the hard young eyes, blue as the mother's, was as disconcerting to Alexis as finding an enemy in the house of a beloved friend.

Her name was Norma, but Alexis privately experimented with names closer, he thought, to her beauty: Andrea, Josephine, Maria. Yet one evening when he came to the table and heard "Norma" spoken, it was as though all the bells in Paris were ringing a sound sweeter than any other.

They were speaking of her, it seemed, because the child was there alone. And what a ridiculous fuss they made over him! They laughed at his remarks and wooed his sulky attention so well, in fact, that his baleful looks were directed toward Alexis no more than twice during the dinner. Indeed, with his mother absent, he seemed inclined to ignore Alexis altogether.

Regretting now that he could not himself speak more casually to the boy, Alexis wondered why no one had asked the question uppermost in his mind: Where was she? Was she ill, perhaps? Or had the father come from America and taken her already to bed?

"Robin, isn't your pretty mother coming to dinner?" Alexis was so absorbed in his own questioning, he'd scarcely heard when one of the guests asked this.

"Nah—" This Alexis heard well enough when Robin answered, his voice shrill with temper. "She's gone out with old cousin Janet Thompkins."

"Well, aren't you the brave boy to stay alone!" exclaimed the woman, but with an odd note, less than sympathetic, in her voice. "But aren't you glad she's having fun with another grownup for a change?"

"It's okay," said the boy with distaste, as though he had heard this argument before and did not like it. Then he burst out, "No, I'm not glad! What can I do all by myself in this dirty, stupid old city?"

"Why, lots of things," said the woman, calmly sitting back with the satisfaction of one who has made a point.

"When is your daddy coming over, Robin?" someone else asked, and Alexis listened, sitting very still, for the answer.

"He better come quick," said the boy, attacking his artichoke as one tearing off the wings of a butterfly. Then, oddly, he cast one look at Alexis, accusingly, before ignoring everyone for the rest of the meal.

There was a fever in Alexis' brain as he walked past the cafés after dinner that night, the excitement of early summer crowding around him on the streets. The street lamps glowed over the chattering pedestrians, and the little cars

nosed doggedly through the crowds; while under the striped
and brightly colored awnings of the cafés opposite the old
church of Saint-Germain-des-Près, the walks were covered
with tables, chairs clustered around close as the toes on one's
foot. Miraculously, Alexis spotted a just unoccupied round
table off the street at the Café Royal. Three young Americans were racing toward it, but Alexis arrived first and
then sat down with a ridiculous feeling of triumph. He
even looked about to see if his success had been witnessed—
and there behind him sat Norma Andrews!

"Madame!" He was springing to his feet when he saw the
other woman beside her, one with a strong, square face,
large blue eyes, and that air of formidable self-assertion
which had made him most careful of his words in the old
days of diplomatic assignments. She could be the wife of an
American Senator or a Congressman, or even of an Ambas-
sador. "I beg your pardon," he murmured, bowing, and
prepared to sit back down—besides, if he did not, quickly,
the young Americans who were once again bearing down
upon him would snatch the table.

"But won't you join us?" asked Mrs. Andrews, smiling as
though they were old friends, while the woman beside her
regarded him with interest.

"With pleasure!" And Alexis relinquished his table to the
youths.

So it was in a moment of trembling awareness that at last,
he found himself staring into the dreaming, unworldly eyes
of the woman he loved. The creamy transparent skin, the
long, dark, curving eyebrows, the smooth fair brow were
there within touch of his eyes or his hand, or his lips . . .

"Mrs. Thompkins, my cousin from New York and Vir-
ginia," she said, with a gay flip of her hand. "Janet, Count
Gronsky. Her husband is a Senator—"

Ah, his instinct had been sound!

"I have met your Senators in my own country," he said politely. "My admiration is great for your American system of government, Madame."

"Now that's the kind of thing my husband would like to hear you say," boomed Mrs. Thompkins, laughing as though she'd made a joke. "The point is, I don't know a darned thing about government, and couldn't care less, Count Gronsky! What I'd like to know is, what does a worldly European like you think of us American females?"

In a prettier woman this might have sounded coquettish, or had Norma Andrews asked, Alexis might have fallen to his knees then and there. As it was, the question was so frank and the woman's face so openly curious that Alexis could speak to her almost as to another man, although of course he did not say the same things.

"I find American women more varied than the leaves of the trees," he said, fervently. "All types, all beautiful—and all kind." This was said with determined gallantry, and Norma smiled.

Mrs. Thompkins laughed outright. "We're all types and sizes, right enough. But Norma, what a charming man!" she said, turning to her cousin with obvious pleasure, something shrewd and amused in her expression as though she had already guessed what Alexis really meant. Norma smiled demurely, but said nothing. "The drinks are on me," said Mrs. Thompkins, and called a waiter.

"Oh, no," protested Alexis, for fortunately he had been paid that day.

"The first ones, anyway," she insisted. "Now—tell me, Count Gronsky, do you have any other name we can use? I could get a complex using that fine title all the time!"

"My name is Alexis," he informed them. "I should be very pleased if you would so address me." How easy it was to achieve *bonhomie* in the American way, he thought, delightedly, and he looked at the Andrews woman, wondering if she would enter into this familiarity with her cousin.

"Alexis," she said, softly, and for a butterfly instant their eyes met and held. "I like that better, too."

"Tell us more about ourselves," insisted Janet Thompkins, gaily, but Norma gently shook her head.

"Let Alexis tell us about himself," she said, as her knee brushed his under the tiny table.

Alexis felt such a start of desire that he made an ineffective and perhaps rash play for her hand below the tabletop, but the woman, although she kept smiling, drew away. For an instant, he feared he had startled her.

"About myself?" What could he say that would interest them? he asked. What could there be about the old ways of his life equal to the fine, exciting world they knew at home in America? New things were important, old things were dull, and should be forgotten. But they kept asking questions and he admitted, after a time, that his past was one of which he could speak with pride. Yes, he had followed in the footsteps of his ancestors, whose influence in his country's history had been in the great tradition. Yes, he had once owned great estates in his homeland, hunting-lodges and rushing waters and miles of fields whose pheasants met their glorious end upon his table. And great balls—ah, yes, with the crystals in the candlelight gleaming like stars and the waltz music catching at the heart so one whirled and whirled with happiness.

But now, he said with solemnity, fearing he had sounded boastful, now they must know he worked for the Americans.

"Of all things!" exclaimed Janet.

"I didn't know that," said Norma, as though she knew other things about him which he had not suspected. "Then some day you must come to the United States, particularly since you speak the language so well. You might even become an American!"

"Is it so easy then to become an American?" he asked, delightedly. They laughed and agreed that it was, it was as easy as that, and he must plan now, from this instant, to come. "But that is already my dream," he assured them. "There are only a *few* obstacles in the way—"

For a moment the Senator's wife regarded him thoughtfully. "Well," she said, "perhaps you'll be clever enough to find a way around those." For an instant he was uncomfortable, wondering what she thought he meant, but right away she called the waiter again and ordered more drinks. This time he would not let her pay for them even though she was a big, hearty woman who apparently liked to drink a great deal, but since she was obviously fond of Norma, Alexis could excuse much. In fact, the longer they sat there, the more fortunate the occasion seemed, and at one point Janet leaned across the table, looking as wise as Guido when he spoke of what he knew, and said that perhaps she might find a way to help him when the time came.

After this, the evening became a reckless succession of cafés and drinks and laughter and keeping up with Janet's energetic curiosity about everything in Paris. When they left the square before the old church, they stopped at another bistro a block away, and after that Janet insisted they descend some stairs into a cellar where the light was too dim and the room so full of smoke they could scarcely see each other. Alexis did not feel quite right bringing them into a place like this, and soon persuaded them to leave, and they found another café, another table under the stars.

Norma did not drink as freely as her cousin but she was feeling it. Her soft body became sinuously flexible and her movements, when they walked arm in arm down the street, seemed consciously seductive. In the flickering lights her red

lips seemed curved with promise, and her voice rose and fell
in such gentle rhythms, ending as it did in a gay and rising
laugh that he thought: Oh, no, she is not always the woman
in control she has seemed beside her child, but warm and ap-
proachable, excitingly provocative, with a gift for love. . . .

It was the instant he thought this, however, that the dirty
little beggar boy threw himself in the street at their feet to
snatch the butt of a cigarette Janet Thompkins had thrown
away. With the practiced ease of a diver for pennies, he
came up with the cigarette in his mouth and Norma shuddered, clasping her hands together, remembering. "Oh,
Janet, I must get back to Robin!"

"Nonsense," said Janet. "That spoiled darling of yours
can jolly well take care of himself for one night!"

"But I know he's waiting up for me—I've left him much
too long!" And one white hand curved nervously around
her beautiful throat.

"Norma, it's been years since I've had such fun as this,"
Janet said sharply. "I'll bet you haven't had any fun either
since you came to Paris!"

"It's not as simple as that," pleaded Norma, and her arm
seemed cold as Alexis took it tenderly in his hand. "*You*
know how his father is—"

How? Alexis would have liked to ask. But, of course, he
could not take part in this conversation, stranger that he
was.

"Sure I know," said Janet. "After all, he is *my* cousin,
isn't he? It only takes half an eye to see what goes wrong
between you two . . ."

But instead of going on, Janet snapped her fingers and
began humming a song they'd heard on the T.S.F. in the
bistro they had just left. "As for me, I'm ready to stay out
all night with Alexis, if he's game!" And she seized his arm
in a not unpleasant hold against her breast. "Romantic

Alexis," she crooned. There was no doubt about it, now she was very drunk and amorous indeed.

Suddenly, recklessly, Norma laughed, and even her flesh seemed to warm under Alexis' hand as she took a small dancing step at his side. "Well, where *do* we go now?" she cried.

It was a long time after that before she again spoke of the child.

The crowds had begun to disperse when they took a table in the last café on their wanderings. A scowling, black-browed proprietor looked as though he would like to close the place, yet he could not bring himself, it seemed, to say no to the American women. So they could choose any table they liked, and be happily by themselves in the semi-privacy of an abandoned bar. Alexis could understand now why American men were so confident and aggressive, so sure they were rulers of the world—these women, flattering, admiring, charming, had the skills to please a man equalled, he thought, only by those from his own country who had beauty famous over all the world.

There was no clear-cut moment when the knowledge came to Alexis that Norma would come to him that night, unless it was when he caught a look between the women which said, plainly enough in any language, "He is yours and waiting." Norma had even blushed, and frowned at Janet. Then both seemed to smile on him like mothers, and Norma's eyes softened as a woman's in love, her beauty so compelling that Alexis could scarcely breathe, thinking of her lying in his arms, and what he would show her of love and passion before the night ended and the next dawn came. He was glad he had learned well this particular skill early in life, for he had been told by Guido of the haste and clumsiness of the American male. He would be gentle with her in love, and slow, so slow . . .

No more, no more, he told himself, in bright spirits. No man dare think beyond that!

He was, however, aware that this cousin of Norma's had the power to bring protocol and disapproval into their beautiful relationship if she sobered enough to do so, and quickly he ordered more brandy. Janet's smile grew coarse, like a peasant's he noticed, showing she too had her moments of lust, and he took her hand gently, even though she was not for him and she knew it, but this enabled him then to take Norma's hand as well.

"Oh, Alexis, I can't drink any more," said Norma, sighing, and dropped her head limply against the back of the red leathercloth seat. Her black hair was an untidy cloud around her brow, and the red lips were touched with moisture from her tongue. "May I have some coffee? It will keep me awake, but I don't care. Not tonight, I don't care about anything tonight when everything tastes so good."

Ah, the taste. Taste was part of love—already her senses were stirred, and soon she would have the taste of his lips on hers. It was almost unendurable to be so conscious of a woman—and Alexis, in sudden alarm, reined in his thoughts. He had been too long alone to consider all this quite rationally now. Yet he must choose with care the first bold moment for the important move, the stage well set, romance sweet and urgent on the air—and he, the strong male in command!

The sky was full of stars as they marched back over the cobblestoned pavement arm in arm and suddenly Alexis burst out in a great hunting-song of his youth. The cousin exclaimed in pleasure, and Norma leaned against him as though his voice had quite taken her breath and strength away. Quickly he changed his song to a waltz tune and caught her about the waist to whirl through the steps of a great ballroom there in the empty Paris street.

The lights of the boulevard were remote, as they danced toward the park with its heavy-laced trees overhead, full of murmur and fragrance. For a moment the intoxicated Janet clung to Alexis also, so that the three of them were waltzing crazily together, laughing and unsteady on their feet until Janet let go again, and he was left alone with Norma in his arms.

Surely Janet could not fail to see that it was time for her to leave; yet the woman caught Norma's arm, and for an instant it seemed she was a possession they would fight over. Then Janet drew away and went wandering ahead with uncertain steps, laughing out loud. He looked down at Norma's sweet face lifted to his, her eyes half-closed, her lips parted and soft as love. Instinct told him what he wanted to know: The moment was here.

"Norma," he whispered. "Lovely Norma—" How beautiful her name was, after all! "Do you feel the strangeness of this night? Does it say to you the things it says to me?" He spoke so softly she could still pretend he said nothing if she wished, but by her small embarrassed laugh, looking away as a young girl (desiring touch first and words after) he knew that she had heard. "My heart is burning with love," he whispered, and she did not draw away when his hand brushed then, as by an accident, across her breasts.

He withdrew his hand at the next moment only because his own breath had come with such a painful rush of desire. Yet how young he must be still to feel that way!

"Where do you wish to go, Janet? Where may we take you?" he asked the cousin when he could speak sensibly again, trying to feel cool and independent as though he had many choices for the night, that he was not as moved as the ladies might believe.

"I have a room at the pension," said Janet, thoughtfully, and he rejoiced, for thus only he and Norma would return to the hotel. To her room or his?

Norma yawned suddenly and a gust of gaiety recurred like wind from a returning storm, carrying them along toward the fountain beside the old Luxembourg wall, and there they heard the song. It was a pulsing of young girls' voices, and as they approached the fountain they saw three figures in white sitting on the high rim. They were singing like sirens, in tones of despair and hope and longing, calling men to love and destruction. The girls' heads were close together and below them stood two youths, their faces also raised, tense and listening. From apartment windows overlooking the park, men and women leaned out to listen as the water splashed in the fountain.

When the song ended, a shout from a window high above their heads demanded more, and the singers began a livelier tune about a naughtier love, and it was hard to imagine any world but this July night in Paris when youth and darkness and the heat of desire brought lovers together under the stars. The American women had become silent, the cousin nodding her head and patting her foot softly in time to the music, while Norma leaned forward as though fearful the moment might escape her. Alexis, feeling his own heart beat, waited only for the moments to come.

The singing girls ended with a burst of sudden laughter and a slap as the girls, human now and lusty, leaped from the fountain rim and tore off up the street, the boys pursuing. Laughter echoed from the sides of gray stone houses and a woman's voice cried, *"C'est la vie, mes enfants! C'est la vie!"* A baby's sudden cry came thinly from a dark window opening below.

Alexis leaned over to look into Norma's eyes, wanting to share everything, knowing she would feel as he did now, that the world was rocking on a wave of love. Oddly, she looked away, frowning, her body no longer swaying with any rhythm.

"Norma," he whispered, his voice strong with urgency. "Norma, let me hold you—"

For a long, disturbing moment she did not answer, but stared at him as a woman, coming out of ether, is shocked to find she has been living in a dream.

I cannot permit this, Alexis told himself, sternly. This prologue has continued too long. I should have brought her back to the hotel hours ago, taken her in my arms at the moment of our desire, and made love to her at once.

"Janet, what do you suppose has happened to Robin? Oh, quickly, I must go back!"

But the cousin now was moving her big body in sensual rhythm, her eyes half closed and her hands held out to Alexis.

"Forget the little bastard, Norma, for once—. He's all right. I feel bad, honey, like doing things no good woman ought to do. That singing—Paris—Alexis—" She moaned, like a woman suddenly gone out of her mind.

It was utterly confusing and Alexis wondered if an American man, in such circumstances, would know what to do. There was his beloved walking coolly some distance away, and when he caught up with her, touching her bare arm, she shivered. And here was Janet, whom he did not desire, leaning her head against his shoulder and saying things he did not wish to hear.

Angrily he kept hold of Norma's arm, even when she stopped at their hotel, even though she tried to draw away.

"You take Janet to the pension," she said, looking up anxiously toward the window of her room. And Janet caught his arm against her full breast and leaned over and kissed Norma. Kissed Norma!

"I'll take Alexis," laughed Janet, "if you're giving him up!"

Fortunately pride saved Alexis from speaking angrily on the street before their hotel. In a moment he was walking stiffly away with Janet, whom he detested, knowing Norma would be let into the lobby alone in answer to her ring, and wondering if this insult to his manhood had been intended all through the summer evening.

At the gate to the pension, Janet did just as he might have expected: she leaned against him heavily, raising her homely honest face. Of course he had to respond, with loathing in his heart.

But she was more sensitive than she seemed and drew back quickly, mocking herself.

"I'm something, Alexis, you know that? Good Lord, look at me! What would Herbert's constituents say? But you're a good egg." She was nodding her head with drunken assurance, although not releasing him. "God knows what you must think of teasing American women, though. I may be drunk, but I wouldn't do that to a man. Norma is a fool!" Then she became brisk and almost sober. "She's always been like that, hot, then cold—Don't *you* feel bad about it." And before he could answer she had disappeared inside the pension gate.

His pride further outraged that she had understood his rejection, Alexis walked with sharp, angry steps back to the hotel with only a brief gratitude that Janet had condemned the younger woman and would herself have gone to bed with him if he had wished. . . .

Yet, just as he reached the corner of his block, he thought suddenly: Perhaps we are both wrong! Perhaps Norma is more clever than either of us, not wanting her husband's cousin to see what she wishes to do. After all, with our rooms one floor above the other—his above!—and the cousin far away, locked up in the pension until tomorrow morning, we do not have to answer to anyone.

Looking up from the street before he rang for the concierge he saw no light. This did not surprise him. Norma was no doubt undressing in the dark, fearing the light would arouse the son who slept in the adjoining room.

But when Alexis climbed the stairs to her door, there was only silence, even when he edged very close and waited; then he heard the key turn sharply in the lock, closing her inviolably within. Yet if one moment before he had tried that door, what then?

The child must be sleeping in her bed, Alexis thought sensibly. It was possible that he had tired of being alone. Then she might come to him on the floor above. He was not a man to mistake a woman's desire, Alexis told himself, his confidence coming back. Norma had let him see her feelings all too well throughout the evening to leave him doubting now. So he waited, wishing to tell her which creaking step to avoid on the stairs, but she still delayed; and, finally, he went on wondering, until the Paris dawn spread dully against his yellow ceiling, which clue he had missed, how he had been so wrong.

It was at the first light of day he heard her moving stealthily below and knew that she had not been sleeping either, perhaps was still waiting for him to act. He got out of bed this time without bothering to be quiet or careful. She must know he still desired her, suffered to take her in his arms. Yet as he stood on the floor his bones ached in an irrelevant way, and there was a dry, alcoholic taste in his mouth.

Dressing before he went down, Alexis put on his gray workday suit and clean white shirt, brushed his hair carefully with the family-crested brushes, and then, for one brief moment, hesitated before the glass. He would be dull at business today, he thought, and the Americans, unlike the French, never excused a man's dull wits for reasons of love.

Yet as he descended the one flight of stairs, his heart again racing, a cold but very small anger held him back an instant. Possibly his position was more ridiculous than before; yet wasn't it mainly for his self-respect that he *must* now go on?

He was about to step up to her door and knock, softly of course, when the one from the adjoining room opened and the boy came out. His red hair was like the rumpled wig of a clown under the dim hall light, his eyes were swollen with sleep and bad temper, and, with no look of recognition whatever, he slid past Alexis into the narrow doorway of the toilet where he seated himself without bothering to close the door. His pajamas hanging in disorder around his feet he stared at Alexis, and apparently deciding they had both come out in the early dawn for the same purpose, grinned mockingly as though he had bested an enemy.

Shocked with this final insult, Alexis rapidly descended the stairs and went out into the cool Paris morning. The old woman from the café next door was already on her way to market, and a young man came around the corner bearing loaves of freshly baked, brown-crusted bread. A mongrel dog barked from across the street, and a large rat slid by in the gutter, but there was no one in all the city of Paris who cared, this morning, for the bitter awakening of an exile from love.

He had foolishly paid another week in advance at the pension, and now he had little money left. He must therefore return for the rest of that week for lunch and dinner, too, no matter what the effort cost him. He would not look at Norma Andrews or her cousin, he resolved, and perhaps the boy would ignore him if Alexis paid no attention to his mother.

Yet when he entered the room at lunch, Janet Thompkins, dressed in a flowery printed silk, was telling those at the table about the night before. Norma was hovering over her child and Alexis sat down in the midst of this recital with all the bright, curious eyes upon him as though he alone might provide the kind of diversion they seemed searching for. Only Mlle du Coeur had the grace to look mildly disapproving.

"Alexis was a wonderful guide," babbled Janet in her loud, bright American voice, and it seemed she would go on forever talking, talking, talking. Then, unexpectedly, she fell silent."That's wrong," she said, quietly, her eyes upon him. Since she had created an audience she seemed to feel impelled to go on, but a reluctance had come into her speech. "Alexis wasn't a guide. He was the most delightful host and the jolliest companion I have ever known."

Scornfully he thought, she cannot flatter me now. But he smiled back tensely, saying nothing, hating them all—and it seemed to him surprising that the same look was in the eyes of Mademoiselle as she looked about her table and then at him.

"Oh, Mr. Gronsky, take us out some night, won't you?" begged Miss Smith, a most aggressive looking woman at the far end of the table. Then others chimed in, as though he were paid to do such things, as though a woman had the right to commandeer a man!

"With pleasure," he said, smiling largely, his teeth clamped together, his manners perfect, but his eyes as rejecting as a locked door.

Norma had said nothing until now. "I didn't sleep very well after, though," she complained, the lines tense and weary on her face. "I drank such a lot of coffee—I might have known what it would do to me. But I hate to have to think of practical things when everyone else is having fun."

She looked at him pleadingly, but he turned from her and began eating the food on his plate. Did she actually think he would sympathize, or ever again trust that look of sadness and desire? No, it gave him satisfaction to see how lack of sleep and perhaps her own tensions had put a grayness on her skin, making her resemble a clay figure beginning to harden in the mold.

Yet the sum total of her character was not in her face at all, he decided, nor were the component parts what they had first seemed. She was not submissive, not gentle nor kind—not like a woman from the old world, thought Alexis, daring then to look at her. Yet when their eyes met she smiled almost teasingly, as though they had been lovers the night before, or could be, another time. Did she not yet understand that a European like Alexis, once rejected, is gone forever? Perhaps that is how American men are different, he thought, with scorn: They give up freedom for too little in return.

No, he would not even accept the gift of her now!

The boy yawned repeatedly over his food, and Norma said in a routine way that Robin had still been awake when she got in last night. They must make up for it tonight. But Robin said he did not intend to go to bed early, he was going to a movie, maybe he'd find himself a new friend. "*You* did," he said, accusingly.

"Oh, Norma," said Janet Thompkins, crossly. "I had hoped we might lure Alexis to go with us tonight as our guest. After all, I leave Paris tomorrow."

"I am so sorry," said Alexis, quickly. "Tonight I am not free."

Norma had already turned back to Robin, who was resentful and sullen. Even though he did not look at Alexis as he answered her small, wooing voice and her absent-minded sweetness, the boy was irritable and ungrateful, monstrous as before . . .

Monstrous? No. It was not so. Suddenly Alexis saw, not the child's rudeness or his selfish, petulant demands upon his mother, but a frightened, lonely, small-boy need of assurances she did not give, of love and generosity that were not in her. The boy was no more a monster than Alexis had been last night, wanting kindness and her love, for there were needs in both man and boy to sicken one if a woman did not understand.

A woman from the old country understands these things from birth, he thought, angrily. Then it came to him like a crystallization of something long kept fluid in his mind: that compassion for the foreignness of man was not in the character of those from the New World at all. There were still two worlds, the old and the new; and only one of these could be his.

It was then, with no outward sign upon his face, that Alexis dropped his eyes from the bright deception of the future to the diminishing certainties of the past, and, at that moment, felt his heart grow old.

Death in a
Beauty Parlor

It was puzzling that one should remember having seen the woman at all, and inconceivable that she should be so sharply printed on the mind from a chance encounter of the day before. Stout and middle-aged and French, with graying hair coarse as country tweed, there was no reason why she should be more memorable than a hundred others; yet the heavy, slow-moving figure crossing the Boulevard Raspail, a Paisley scarf pinned high at the neck of a shapeless black dress, had the familiarity of a presence one passed every day in one's life.

Ellen said nothing of this to the child as, holding fast to Francie's hand, she maneuvered her off the street and into the clamorous market-day crowd, banishing the woman from sight and surely, this time, from the mind.

" 'Allo, 'allo," cried a sidewalk merchant from the dim interior of his stall (dim only because the sunlight was so bright above). *"Regardez les poissons, Madame!"* They looked up at his large face rosy as the pink *langoustes* he'd boiled in salt water from the sea, and playfully he pretended to throw a shrimp at Francie who giggled as Ellen hurried her on. The market this morning was bright as one of the child's own paintings: purple cèpes large as monk's caps, giant beets split and staining blood-red a bed of old newspapers, white cauliflowers pyramided like the skulls in the Catacombs; and tiny, Dresden-pretty bouquets of fresh flowers covered an entire stand. . . . There were *moules* from Portugal with whiskers like old sea-dwarfs, beans long and green and succulent as spring, and green parsley was mounded up from the pavement high as a garden wall. A butter and cheese stand smelled like a damp-bottomed baby, and nearby red-combed chickens cackled and beat their wings against their final hour; while over all was the fragrance of ripe sweet fruit, tempting as the apple must have been to Eve.

The little girl squealed when a pile of oranges fell cascading to her feet, and she and two women shoppers stooped to help retrieve them for the vendor. Then others fell, until all was confusion among the jostling, good-natured housewives, the merchant shouting out his dismay until most of the fruit was placed back upon the stand. Then with a splendid gesture, he handed Francie the largest orange in sight and once more happily renewed his cry: *"Oranges d'Afrique, Mesdames, Messieurs! Pas chères, ils ne sont pas chères!"*

Ellen bought some plums and purple grapes at another stand and Francie asked for a pomegranate for its pretty color; all were put in one large cornucopia made from the newspaper, *le Figaro*. By the time they left the market scene, warmed by its homely gaiety, even Ellen's face was flushed and almost relaxed—until she saw Francie had taken out the orange and was holding it in her hand.

"Don't eat that!" she cautioned, sharply. "You can't eat the orange until the skin is washed, Francie, you know that!" In her anxiety, her voice was much too shrill, and when the child regretfully put the orange back in the cornucopia, Ellen felt a moment's regret. She did not want to be afraid of so many things; but there was so much that could happen to a child between the hours of rising and the safe return to her bed, especially in a foreign land. Even after all these months she was still afraid.

It never helped when Lester pointed out they were fortunate his Fulbright scholarship demanded study of Eighteenth Century France in Paris, and not, for example, of some remote tribal customs in darkest Africa. Paris, after all, was the most civilized city in the world, he reminded her, somewhat irritably (perhaps he was not altogether certain of this, himself) ; but Ellen could not quite ignore some of the things she had seen. Doctor's instruments brought out half-sterilized the time Francie had a boil, kitchens which smelled so fragrant, furnished with splintering wood counters and mottled tin pans and refrigerators only half large enough to keep food fresh—and she'd seen a rat running in the street the first day they'd arrived. No, the fruit was not to be trusted until it had been thoroughly washed under running water in their room—but Ellen sighed. So often had she been obsessed by this pain of responsibility, this underlying fear of danger . . . Danger! And her heart thumped as she noticed Francie now held the grapes in her hand, grapes carrying a sediment of poisonous green spray on the twisted stems.

"Francie!" she cried again, and the little girl put the fruit back in the paper without a word, looking up with a disarming smile.

"I know, Mummy," she agreed, the soft round face uncomplaining, the dark hair curling on the small head substantial as Ellen's own hand. The mother, with an unexpected impulse, caught the child against her side.

"Don't you worry, darling!" she cried, feeling unaccountable guilt as Francie once more wistfully touched a finger to the orange; for a gift, in a child's logic, gives only the donor a right to withhold it. Maybe it will be better if I carry the fruit, Ellen thought, but when she saw by a jeweler's clock that she was almost late for her hairdressing appointment one worry replaced the other.

"Oh, we must hurry," she fretted, walking rapidly to the corner of the rue de Rennes, and they did not stop or talk again until they saw ahead of them the blue door and the sign: *Coiffeuse, Mme Darel, Prop.*

Just before they reached the blue door, however, the child turned a moment longer toward the bright noisy street, the gay sounds and cries, and she looked up at her mother as though asking if they might turn back after all. Tentatively as a promise, she lightly touched the big orange with her finger, and Ellen thought, Why do I bother? Lester doesn't really notice how I look. If we went back to the pension now, Francie could eat the orange before lunch. But the blue door was suddenly flung wide and Josette of the skillful hands stood there to admit them. *"Bonjour, Madame,"* she trilled. *"Bonjour, ma petite. Entrez!"* They could not now retreat.

So Ellen led the child into the artificially lighted temple with the enameled basins and chrome-plated chairs, the dryers like helmeted soldiers ranged along the right wall, the manicure tables ready under small white towels for ministration of mesdames' hands and down the length of the room the rows of mirrors, before which clients sat narcissistically for the ritual of being set and combed and finally sprayed with lacquer.

"Where do I sit, Mummy?" asked the child, and Josette, with the quick, loving smile of her kind, swept cotton and wisps of hair and metal pins from the far side of a mirrored table, energetically rubbed the enameled surface with the hem of her blue apron and announced radiantly: *"Voilà, Mam'selle!* You sit here, *ma petite!"*

"Merci, Mam'selle," the child said politely.

"Ah, la petite Americaine, elle parle Français!" exclaimed Josette, calling attention to this phenomenon so that other blue-aproned girls exclaimed also, smiling, pausing in whatever they were doing—but not for long, since Madame Darel had her cold eyes upon them.

The child stared at herself in the mirror with deadly seriousness for a moment or two, then looked around at the customers, an inspection which lasted but a few moments before she settled down with the crayon box her mother had brought along. Selecting a red crayon she solemnly began to draw on the surface of the paper, and finally Ellen could almost relax, seeing the child safe and occupied. As Josette draped the light blue sheet around her shoulders and the strong knowledgeable fingers began manipulating, gently, her scalp and neck, Ellen even permitted herself a measure of contentment. Around them, the operators darted on high-heeled wedgies, their blue aprons cinched in at their waists, and the dryers roared as the air grew heavy with sulphur and ammonia fumes rising from permanent waving and bleaching hair. She saw the girls lean over their clients with eyes tightly focused on their tasks, blinking sometimes from the fumes and too-close air, and was reassured by the thought: this was a good shop. Most women went out looking better than when they had come in, and the simple set she had on her own hair was not expensive: Ellen worried always about money spent away from home.

It was at this moment that she again saw the dowdy Frenchwoman, seated in the next chair but one to hers. The Paisley scarf was still in place, and, although the wide cheekbones were no longer pale, the tweedy hair and small babyish features were unmistakably the same she'd seen the day before and on the street earlier that morning.

If the woman were a fellow American Ellen would surely, this time, have spoken to her of the coincidence. "Imagine," she would have said, "our meeting three times in two days!" This is how she would have spoken at home to a stranger and for a moment she felt glad to be returning soon to Schenectady. There, the woman would have responded in the friendly way of most Americans: "Extraordinary, yes! I remember you also—and your charming little girl." (People always did remember Francie.)

The Frenchwoman was actually smiling now, but rather oddly, a smile which might have been meant for anyone; still, as their eyes met in the long gleaming mirror Ellen leaned slightly forward to speak. "Madame," she began, but the woman gave no sign of recognition. Ellen sat back. From her mirror she could see the gray hair being put up on its rollers—half up and half down, it hung like the ravelings of an old woolen shawl—and in the neonlighting she seemed much older, but it was the same face, the same body, the same large swollen hands now held on the woman's lap (Ellen had not thought she'd noticed these before). "Madame, please excuse me," she went on, doggedly. "It's odd we meet again," she said, telling herself that beauty salons were the same the world over and that all women are equals stripped of their small vanities. "I couldn't resist speaking," she hurried on, wanting to say too, that it was a coincidence, but not certain how to say this well in French. But the woman only turned her head slightly and said through the still smile, "*Je ne comprends pas.*"

She had refused contact; and Ellen, in embarrassment, quickly picked up a magazine and began turning its pages.

Poor Marie was having a dreadful time with the woman's hair, she saw a moment later in the mirror, although the strange woman made no protest under the girl's increasingly irritated hands. Her hair would not stay on the curlers or in pins either, and the girl looked first cross then sullen, for by the time one curl was done, the curl she'd made before was pushing out until Marie had poured most of a bottle of lotion over it. Surely this was enough to make a girl weep; and Marie showed her despair as she glanced around at the other operators, until Madame Darel frowned a warning and turned her back, pointedly, on Marie's problem. But finally, by the time Ellen had been shampooed and was back in her chair, the job was finished and Marie was resolutely fastening a pink net over the large passive head with the speed and finality of clamping down a butterfly. Then straightening up, her hands to her back muscles as though she'd been undergoing great physical strain, she led the acquiescent woman to a dryer against the blue right wall.

"*Ici, Madame,*" she said coldly, and the woman let herself be fixed in the leatherized chair, the set smile on the big mouth remaining even when she was under the hood shut off from voices and other sounds in the room.

Ellen looked up to see Francie beside her, waiting patiently with a drawing which she would naturally expect to have praised. But as Ellen said brightly, "Very pretty, Francie," the child turned straight away into the mask of that fixed, false smile of the woman, a brief worry shadowing her face. She even inclined her small vertical body forward as though she had been spoken to, or perhaps summoned before she turned away to walk in her precise child-manner around the mirrored table back to her own place. Then once again she was hidden from her mother's sight.

Ellen, wondering what the child had seen, looked back at the woman and met her eyes again, so deeply tragic now in the rigid frame of the machine that it occurred to her perhaps nothing from without could ever penetrate the woman's thoughts; in spite of her uneasiness, she felt a stab of pity, which she rejected the next instant.

But at last she relaxed under Josette's hands as her own faded blonde hair went smoothly into the rollers. Then Marie came up and she and Josette talked about the woman, who would not be able to hear their words with the drier roaring in her ears. She lived somewhere in the neighborhood, they said, and she was often strange; no one had ever been able to get much out of her, where she lived, whether she had a family, who she was. Perhaps one should pity her, but it was hard to feel sympathy for someone so unresponsive. Maybe she was crazy.

"I tried to speak to her," said Ellen, and they nodded, saying it had been very kind of her to do so, and that the woman had never been quite as strange as she was today. Even her hair was less manageable, said Marie, and they cast looks of scorn at the creature now fastened in so snugly under the dryer it seemed she could perhaps not have moved had she tried. Like a mummy beneath that metal hood, she scarcely resembled a human being—and wouldn't you think under that heat she'd loosen the Paisley scarf from around her neck?

Ellen's hair was finished with a flourish in which even Madame Darel participated, then she was led like visiting royalty to her chair under her drying machine. They handed her a copy of *Elle* Magazine and she relaxed, thinking that at such moments it was not too bad being in a foreign land, so long as Francie was safely in sight across the room. She could see the child now, absorbed in her drawing, so she closed her eyes and dozed briefly, the magazine held lightly in her hands.

Then something happened. It was hard to tell how first one knew, but when Ellen opened her eyes Josette was exclaiming and pointing to the French woman under the dryer while Marie went swiftly over, stooping to speak, to ask if Madame were all right. . . . When there was no answer, Marie began slapping the woman's wrists and then her cheeks before she drew back wildly looking for Madame Darel.

The woman was still smiling, Ellen observed nervously, her eyes bright open, and she was not pale; but as Marie dropped the hand it fell with a stiff, queer thud as though responding to some final force of gravity. She was unconscious! Yet in a way, even this was simply an exaggeration of how she had been before, and it all happened so swiftly that no one became really alarmed until Madame came briskly forward and lifted off the hood. Then the woman's body fell slowly forward.

Madame Darel, calm as an actress who has been part of many such performances before, pushed back the unresisting head against the chair and almost matter-of-factly clamped down the hood again. This time the woman's brow rested against the frame of the dryer and from the strangely mottled face her dark, sunken eyes stared sightlessly into the room.

"*Cherchez quelqu'un!*" Madame sharply commanded Marie, then irritably admonished the other girls to return to their tasks, since they were being paid "to work, *pas à voir, n'est-ce pas?*"

Some of the other customers had also become aware of the strange happening, so it was necessary that Madame go about the room explaining that "*cette cliente*" had suffered a customary "*faiblesse,*" but that they must not be concerned, it had happened before. She then complimented one girl on a manicure, and a customer on the color of her recently dyed hair, while the poor operators in their blue, tight-waisted aprons busied themselves at their tasks to avoid the scolding looks she gave them.

Marie had run out into the street obediently, the blue door closed behind her; for a long-held moment, all seemed calm. Once again Ellen became aware of the sounds of the machines, of the familiar complex smells and the neon lighting overhead. Then her heart lurched to see Francie looking around the corner of her table with a bright stare of curiosity at the woman's face—although thank God, the mirrors surely had made a screen during that awful moment just before; and when Francie caught her mother's eyes and smiled most naturally, even somehow reassuringly, Ellen saw she had been frightened by nothing, after all. Motioning the child to stay where she was, signalling too that her hair was almost dry, she was further reassured when Francie went back to her coloring, and another moment passed.

Suddenly, rudely, the blue street door war flung open and two men, following Marie, hurried into the room. Their dark suits and sallow faces under winter felt hats were incongruous in such surroundings as they came up to Madame Darel, who tossed her head almost indifferently toward the immobilized woman; but, resourceful as ever, she picked up a straight chair and the three converged upon the inert figure waiting under the hot, still roaring dryer.

Briskly raising the hood in perfect teamwork, the two men lifted the woman into the straight-backed chair as the Paisley scarf twisted further around her neck. One man held the flat of his hand against her big bosom to keep her upright, and it was all done so quietly one could believe this was something for which they had rehearsed on the street outside before being called inside the shop.

Madame Darel, keeping close beside them, talked rapidly and reassuringly over her shoulder to the clients, who could all now very plainly see that something was terribly wrong. "Madame often has the spells," she assured them again, firmly, while Ellen prayed that Francie would keep busy until the chair with its awful burden was carried away. She herself felt suddenly faint, and for a moment thrust up her own dryer-hood, pretending that this was the reason, that she had become too warm. But she was trembling, trapped for the moment, almost ill.

Perhaps the event would have ended there if one of the men had not looked back contemptuously on all of them— those in the blue uniforms and the more pampered ones with bodies draped, their faces scared, exposed; and he tossed his head.

"Cette dame n'est plus du monde!" he said in a loud voice. *"Elle est morte!"* and horribly he lifted the dark-skinned right hand, letting it fall back hard onto the woman's stiff lap. He then outrageously pressed one thumb upon an eye-lid so that one eye was closed, the other left open staring, indecently flirtatious. Even Madame Darel shuddered and cried out for them to go, flinging the door open wide upon the street and urging them to go faster with their burden.

A sigh and a shudder seemed to rise from every woman from every corner of the shop as though all were now involved in this farce, this tragedy, this death of one of their own sex. One young woman with a white foaming bleach just applied to her hair snatched off the blue sheet and began hysterically pulling on her gloves to leave until Madame Darel ran back and soothed her, dissuaded her, got her to sit down again while a weeping Josette gently massaged her tense and straining neck.

Although it was incredible that anyone in the room could have remained uninvolved, Ellen had seen Francie glance around only once, then, apparently utterly absorbed in her drawing, she turned back to it, after a falsely reassuring look from her mother. Ellen felt like crying with relief. But in another moment the child put aside her drawing things and went to the door to peer out through the curtains. Surely the woman had been carried away by then; and briefly Francie sought her mother's eye as though asking a question which gave Ellen a chance to nod reassuringly. There could be no problem now. The shop was seemingly returned to normal, with most of the women again leafing through magazines, the girls absorbed in other heads of hair, and Madame Darel standing officiously once more behind her cash register. The child continued to stare through the door a moment longer, then moved back out of sight.

In another ten minutes Ellen's hair had been combed and lacquered and they were walking down the rue de Rennes, the street bright as before, the hawkers' voices shouting still in the distance. Noonday crowds were hurrying past carrying loaves of bread and small packages of meat or lettuce or legumes in string bags, their faces set in home directions, and Ellen, glancing down on Francie's small dark bobbing head, realized that the child must be hungry. They would have to hurry to reach the pension in time for lunch.

"You must be hungry, Francie," she said, worriedly; and it was then she noticed that the newspaper cornucopia seemed smaller, lighter, less full. With a throb of her heart, she seized the paper from the child's hand so violently that the package split open and the orange, the plums and the apples scattered over the sidewalk. Even the pomegranate fell; but where were the grapes? Only the poisonous stems with the green seedlings were left—

"Francie, where are the grapes? You disobeyed me!" she cried. Catching the child roughly by the shoulders while an elderly Frenchman frowned on such public embarrassment of a child she begged, "You *didn't* eat them. Oh, you *couldn't*—Francie, you didn't eat the grapes, did you?"

The child stood very still, her small jaw stubbornly resisting, until at her mother's continued entreaty she began to cry.

"You said, yes! You wouldn't look at me," she said. "You just looked at her. I asked you, I *did*. I showed you the little grapes and your head went *yes*. I wouldn't eat the orange the man gave me, I told you I wouldn't eat the orange!" Then almost coldly she looked up at Ellen. "You wouldn't look at anything but that old dead lady!"

Ellen stared down on the small closed face with the tears on the round pink cheeks and mechanically she asked, "What dead lady, Francie? What are you saying? What do you mean?"

"The *big* dead lady. The one out on the sidewalk, and she went *dead* and they put her in that car. . . . That man took her pocketbook too, and she was *dead*. She can't make him give it back when she's dead, can she, Mummy? Can she?" she repeated, as she pulled on Ellen's hand.

Ellen shook her head blindly as one whose world is out of focus, while around them the curious French faces reproached her because of the spilled fruit on the sidewalk and in the gutter, and two policemen riding past on bicycles cast appraising glances before they stared with wise French faces at the closed blue door of the Salon de Beauté. Then they pedalled on, indifferently, to their own repasts.

Now Francie was stooping in the street, gathering up the plums and apples and the orange, even the pomegranate half-crushed now, wiping each on the front of her little smocked dress before wrapping it again in the torn fragment of the newspaper. Finally, with her arms embracing her clumsy burden, she looked up patiently, questioningly, as though to say, We don't have to be afraid now, do we?

No, Ellen wanted to say. No, Francie, why should we be afraid? But the words did not come, and her trembling did not cease, and her thoughts kept spinning in awful confusion. There really was nothing else she could do, at the moment, but accept the pomegranate that Francie had wiped on her dress and, as a peace offering, was holding out to her.

Judgment in Burgundy

She had met Alexander Crowell that first day when she
came to the pension table and had formed her opinion
of him before the woman introduced as Winifred Smith
could speak. "Our Casanova of the pension," the sharp-
faced woman scoffed an instant later, but by then it was too
late. Joan had already warmed to the big, gray-haired man's
darting glance of inspection, had smiled in return to the
grin on his large snub-nosed face, and had observed Mme du
Coeur's peppery bangs tilted coquettishly, even as she reproached him:

"Ah, once again, M. Crowell, you are late."

"Forgive me, Mademoiselle," Mr. Crowell begged in mock
distress. "It's that blasted Metro, always the Metro! I'll
never be late again, I swear."

"Oh, do you?" asked Winifred Smith with a forced, unpleasant laugh, fingering the green artichoke on her plate.
"Why don't they ever wash these things properly in
France?" she complained an instant later, drawing the thick
base of a leaf savagely between her big front teeth. Mr.

Crowell shot her a look of obvious dislike, then sat down
and ignored everyone for the rest of the meal.

There was silence for a time, as they all devoted themselves to the excellent food. The noonday sun shot pink and
amber rays through the wine bottles on the white cloth,
flickered over the faces of darting bonnes serving each carefully pre-measured portion, and lifted into prominence the
white fichu on an ancestral portrait of a lady of the Revolu-
tion; then Mr. Crowell was on his feet again. Bending over
Mme du Coeur as though he would plant a kiss upon her
brow, he murmured, "A fine *repas, ma chère Mademoiselle.
Ce soir* I will be here, *en avancez!*" With an unexpectedly
raffish wink at Joan, he then strode out of the room with
the air of a man who knows there can never be time enough
for all the exciting things he has to do.

"That man!" scoffed Winifred Smith, and thrust her
spoon mounded with chocolate mousse in and out of her
dark-red lips. "Wherever did *he* learn to speak French?"
She stared after him so resentfully in fact, that Joan was
surprised a few moments later when the woman hurried to
the parlor window to stare down on the courtyard as though
hoping still to keep Alexander Crowell in her sight.

Many who came through Paris during the summer
months settled like ants in the pension, believing it was the
anthill of Paris itself; perhaps, in a way, it was. Returning
from cautious excursions out for cultural food, they could
rest in the reassuring warmth of the Pension du Coeur and
observe, if they cared to, how French efficiency and the
superb illusion of French well-being were maintained by
seemingly amateurish means; but it was difficult to ignore
other Americans, who sometimes managed to spoil it all.

Alexander Crowell, it seemed, had found the solution to
this in his own way. He lived outside the Pension du Coeur

in a small hotel on the rue d'Assas, and came in only for his meals, escaping the moment after. Thus he seemed to find all the exciting things that others missed. Joan wanted to tell him she'd expected more adventures too, but the first week he didn't give her a chance: it was not quite truthful the way she wrote home about him, as if they shared more than they did.

"Mr. Crowell has a fine sense of adventure," she informed one of her fellow teachers at the Westlawn, New Jersey, high school. "You can't imagine all the unusual things he finds for us to do." Again she wrote, "The chestnut trees are in full leaf now, and the little green nuts sometimes fall on one's head," because he had spoken of this amusingly the night before at dinner.

She also wrote home about Winifred, since in travel one sometimes had to settle for what one could get. The woman was amusing at times, when she related the casual gossip of the pension, and she was companionable enough the few excursions they took together; but when she talked about Alexander Crowell, Joan liked her not at all, and from the start had turned away at such moments.

"What's the man running away from?" Winifred would ask. "Trouble, I'll bet." Joan simply would not answer. "Who knitted that silly vest he wears?" Joan ignored this, and other things too, until the day Winifred announced, more challenging than usual, "*Now* that man claims to be a composer!—Some people pretend to be anything away from home!"

"Why on earth would he pretend to be something that he's not?" cried Joan, unable to stop herself.

"Why? To impress idiotic girls like you," retorted Winifred, as though she'd been waiting all along for Joan to come to his defense. "Watch out for that man, my girl. Married or not, he's got plain sex on his brain."

"Good night, Winifred," said Joan, coldly, and went to her room. But she could not help noticing the next day when a blonde girl with high breasts in a magenta sweater was seated next to Alexander Crowell, and how he kept his eyes on her.

"Watch this," said Winifred, nudging Joan, and the woman's smile was triumphant when they left the pension together after dinner, Mr. Crowell sweeping the girl out ahead of him like a young man in the full flower of his youth.

Yet this gave Joan an idea, and the following day she had her brown hair styled at a beauty parlor on the rue de Rennes, and for dinner wore a green dress that dramatized her eyes. That night she flirted quite daringly with Mr. Crowell, who responded at once by asking what she was doing, later. It was as easy as that!

She was about to say, "Nothing at all," when Winifred reminded her that they'd planned to go to the Café Flore for coffee and if they were going to find a table free they'd better start pretty soon. Mr. Crowell left so hastily then, there was nothing Joan could do but follow Winifred.

Later, sitting stiffly at a small table on the Boulevard, sipping black coffee and having a miserable time, Winifred looked enormously pleased with herself. She hugged a heavy sweater across her large breasts and talked of her long divorced husband, in this way showing her scorn of all men. It was at this moment that Mr. Crowell came striding across the Boulevard, heading straight to a table against the wall where a young man stood pointing to a vacant chair beside a beautiful red-haired girl.

"Casanova rides again!—He's too fast for you, Joan," said Winifred, as the girl with the red hair began flirting with Mr. Crowell at once.

"He's not fast," protested Joan, "and who said he's 'for'

me, anyway?" She began gathering up her things in irritated decision. "I'm getting awfully tired hearing you talk about him so much, Winifred. So if you don't mind, I'm going back to the pension to bed."

"*I* talk about him?" The woman sounded genuinely surprised. "Why, it's you who bring his name into the conversation all the time. He's less than dust to me. . . . I'll bet you can't say that," she added, slyly, and when Joan did not answer, she lighted another cigarette as though she would stay here forever. Nor did they leave, until the table with Mr. Crowell and the red-haired girl was lost in darkness and there was nothing more to stay out for on the extravagantly noisy, gasoline smelling, Boulevard St. Germain.

The next day when she came in for lunch, Joan saw Alexander Crowell in the small foyer adjusting his tie before the hatrack mirror. On a chair beside him was a book he'd put down, and a letter on which his name was written in a bold, feminine hand; she could read the return address, "Clifton Heights, Harrisburg, Pa." The bulky shape of the letter indicated that it contained photographs, she thought, with interest.

He grinned at Joan, then unexpectedly asked her: "*You* aren't leaving us now, are you?"

She had been making inquiries that very morning about trips out of Paris, so it was odd that he would ask. Her time in Europe was running short in any case, but more than anything else she had been motivated by her annoyance with Winifred Smith (in some absurd way, she also felt Alexander Crowell was to blame).

"Soon, I think," she said, with a look which he could not possibly have understood; then she relented. "But not until after dinner tonight."

"Good. We can have a talk then," he said, and he really seemed to have something important on his mind.

That evening she left the travel folders in her room, but went to the table with the refreshed feeling of having taken her life back into her own hands.

"Well, what have you been up to?" asked Winifred, staring, but so improved was Joan's state of mind that she did not feel compelled to answer. Instead she leaned forward to hear the conversation between Alexander Crowell and the retired Professor Cook when Mr. Crowell nodded to her without pausing in what he was saying.

"I've wanted to see that Burgundy country ever since I was a kid. Ever since my dad caught me poring over a *National Geographic* Magazine with pictures of French peasants treading grapes; one pretty girl in bare feet had her head tilted back while a boy fed big purple grapes into her mouth. And another—I can see that one, yet!—held a big bunch between her teeth with her skirt up to *here*. That was when my father took the thing away. 'What is the *National Geographic* coming to?' he cried. But by then it was too late to save my thirsty soul. I vowed I'd feed grapes to a pretty girl in Burgundy some day!"

Mrs. Cook giggled, Professor Cook nodded sympathetically, and Joan was about to say she'd always wanted to see that too, when Alexander Crowell turned to her and asked: "Want to come along?"

"Come along?" she asked, and he explained that a young friend of his had offered to drive him and any two friends he chose into the Burgundy wine country for a nine-day trip. "Leaving tomorrow," he said. "Shouldn't be too expensive." So she understood she would be expected to pay her own way, which was fine.

"I'd love to," she said at once, but uneasily conscious that

Winifred had leaned forward too. Then quick as a stroke of lightning, the woman said: "You've room for one more then, so count me in too."

If Alexander Crowell's attention had not been diverted at that moment toward an attractive new girl nibbling on red cherries he would not have been caught off-guard. As it was, he simply did not react quick enough, in spite of Joan's silent plea. He even nodded absentmindedly; then it was too late. Winifred too, would go.

When they started out at four in the afternoon on the following day, the orange chimney pots on old Parisian roofs were like children's pails forgotten in the sun, green chestnuts hung on leafy trees like ornaments, and beneath the trees sturdy red begonias swelled with ripe summer bloom. These sights made artists of them all, until they became uncomfortably aware of the air blue from exhausts on Parisian cars, and Jerry, Alexander's young friend drove in and out with rising temper, cursing all the cars crowding like beetles along the city streets.

The red-haired girl, his wife, loyally cried insulting remarks at those drivers who got in her husband's way—as mercurial a young couple, Joan thought, as she had ever seen. Only Mr. Crowell craned his neck from side to side as though to see everything of Paris before it vanished, and remained cheerful. . . . But finally they were on the Autoroute heading south, the day sunny and the sky clear blue, and only Winifred retained a look of criticism upon her face. It was plain to anyone that she would never trust the young man at the wheel, or his wife who was constantly distracting him. But even she could not stop the rising sense of anticipation in them all.

It wasn't long before they became first names to each other, and the French girl pronounced "Aleex" in fits of laughter as she bounded about in the front seat. Jerry, whose crew haircut was so utterly unsuited to the small, rodentlike face, observed her from time to time with obsessive pride; but very soon it became apparent he was jealous and proud by turns. Françoise laughed, then sulked, four times on the way to Fontainebleau, and twice kissed her husband passionately on his big right ear. There was constant nerve response between the two as with children at play, and Alexander and Joan smiled at them; but Winifred leaned forward listening intently as though each word and gesture had some significance she would store away.

They stopped at Fontainebleau long enough to feed the sluggish, pot-bellied old carp in the palace pond, Alexander sitting stolidly on the abutment tearing apart a loaf of bread while Françoise took photographs of him until Jerry irritably snatched the camera from her hands. From there they drove through the countryside to Moret, a tiny walled city of the Thirteenth Century, crammed with tourists and glutted with their cars; but at a fine inn overlooking the river Loing, Alexander ordered white Burgundy wine and fresh river trout with the excited air of a boy for the first time in his life doing exactly as he pleased.

They took three rooms at the inn, one for the young couple, one for Alexander, and one to be shared by Winifred and Joan. So that after they'd mounted the winding stairs after dinner Joan could not escape Winifred's whispering comments on the probably illegal relationship of Jerry and Françoise. Not for one minute, she said, did she believe they were man and wife because . . . For ten minutes she brought out small indictments of their obviously impermanent relationship, until Joan closed her hands over her ears and said she would listen no more.

It was then, in a strange, excited whisper that Winifred said: "But you'd better listen to this . . . If Alexander

Crowell doesn't stop touching my breast in that car I'm going to scream!"

Joan rose up with startled protest. "How can he avoid touching you, crowded the way he is between us? Honestly, Winifred——"

"So he's touching you too, is he?" said the woman triumphantly, and Joan could do nothing but pull the white hemstitched sheet over her ears and pretend to go to sleep.

Next day they made an early start, going deep into the wine country (but the grapes were still green and small, and many of the vines had just been sprayed with poisonous-looking green or yellow powders). Still they found one beautiful cathedral and more fine food, and they got out frequently to see random sights which gave them some relief from the crowded little car which was not really large enough for five. Sometimes three in the front seat, sometimes three in back—the front seat had more space—they changed about often, only Françoise remaining always in front beside the window. At first Alexander was the one who moved up most often between the couple, but when it became apparent to everyone that the husband was growing jealous, Alexander settled in back and wisely refused to change again; instead, he suggested that Winifred, being so slender, remain in front with them.

That night in their shared room the older woman did not speak of the fine Musigny wine, the Cathedral at Auxerre, the chalk cliffs and the winding river but, in the manner of a child whose idea of insult is Miss-this or Miss-that, said "Well, Miss Joan, you're really working fast now, aren't you? I suppose you put Alexander up to keeping me in front, with all that room in back for just the two of you." Then she added, slyly, "But he's still got his eye on the French girl, you wait and see!"

"I've warned you, Winifred!" stormed Joan, turning her back, but then she did recall a moment when Alexander had helped Françoise from the car and the girl had clung to his shoulder in quick clinging intimacy until he'd drawn away under the jealous eyes of her husband.

They talked about many things as they drove through the green and gentle countryside, so that by the end of the third day they knew a great deal about each other. Jerry had grown up singing in the Mormon Tabernacle choir, even though he was a Roman Catholic who'd perjured himself both ways to get in. Winifred, after divorcing "a cold fish of a man," taught mathematics to small children whose parents caused her no end of trouble and whose fathers invariably made "proposals" to her (she was actually rather a good-looking woman as the sun and air flushed and tanned her cheeks; still, she was too seldom pleased . . .). Once, she related, she'd had to go to a man's wife about his attentions; and suddenly each of the party saw her as a very different being from themselves, too shocked to comment. Only Françoise gave Winifred a startled reproachful look. "That, I would nevair do!" she said simply.

The French girl frequently pouted when the others reached some point of reference alien to her understanding, and would break in loudly with a long story difficult for anyone to follow, in her rapid, excited, French-accented English. But Winifred was wrong: Françoise *was* married to Jerry, and one day she told them how beautiful their wedding had been in the parish church. For five minutes after that she and her young husband held hands tenderly, until he just missed hitting a stray chicken in the road and she began quarreling with him again.

Alex told little of himself, but several times he mentioned his wife, fondly. Shaking his head, once he'd complained that she had absolutely no ear for music and that he'd had to teach her every note she knew. Then, as though he missed her, he fell silent. It was not until the fifth day that he brought out the photos.

In the mood of those who have chosen exile yet suddenly remember matters left behind, they had been wondering when they would again hear from home. "I got my last mail before I left Paris," he said quietly, and took four prints from the enevelope Joan had seen. "My sister sent these to me." There in each was the face and figure of a woman past middle age, wearing an unbecoming hat, glasses, and an apologetic camera smile; but in one snapshot where she was hatless and smiling with Alexander close beside her, she was almost pretty, and he was leaning forward with such a loving, curious look of compassion Joan could find nothing to say.

"That's my wife," he said, and his face seemed to lengthen as though the sun had changed direction. "That's Elaine."

Françoise snatched the photos and held them in exaggerated distance from her eyes.

"Ah, but she is old like your mothair!" she exclaimed, shockingly. "She cannot be your wife, Aleex! Ah, *non, non—*" Still protesting, she turned to her husband to point out this impossibility, but Jerry must have communicated something to her, for with a false smile of politeness she handed the photos back. "Is nice," she said, flatly, carefully. "*Très gentille;* a nice lady," looking to her husband for approval. Alex accepted the photos and put them in his wallet.

"She was—gentle," he said. "She died the day before Easter. These photographs were taken the week before—I'd forgotten I had taken them until I got out my camera for this trip." He was speaking carefully, almost apologetically.

"I'm so sorry," murmured Joan, deeply moved.

"Cancer?" asked Winifred, brightly.

Alexander nodded; and then immediately began talking of other things so they should know he meant for them to forget what he had told them. He seemed to take particular care to appeal to Françoise, and soon they were laughing at the same joke and he reached over and patted the top of her head as though she were a child. To Joan he said little, but it seemed to her their bodies touched more often with the swaying of the car.

That night in their room Winifred did not begin talking as on other nights about the young couple, about Alexander, about her own physical discomfort. She did not even complain about the things she had not cared for, the poisonous-looking spray on the vineyard grapes, the outdoor toilet she'd had to use standing over the porcelain floor, but Joan, glancing at her obliquely, knew Winifred would certainly speak of something unpleasant before they could sleep. Trying to prevent this, for surely it would be some criticism of Alex and his dead wife, Joan said quickly: "I'm so tired— do you mind if we just don't talk tonight, Winifred, and go to sleep at once?"

"No, I don't mind," said Winifred, with an air of cool surprise, and turned off the light; so it was not until five minutes later that she said what it was inevitable from the first that she would say: "Looks like you've got a chance with him after all, doesn't it, Joan? No wife, no morals— it's between you and Frenchie now, I guess."

"Oh, honestly!" exclaimed Joan. "I won't share a room with you another night, Winifred, if you don't stop saying such things. If you don't stop talking about him!" Suddenly it seemed she'd been a fool not to have insisted on being alone, long before.

"I expected you to say that. After all, a room alone? Nobody would know what you were up to then, would

they?" Winifred asked this as brightly as though she were
passing the time of day.

Joan sat up in bed shaking with helpless anger. "You'd
say anything, wouldn't you, anything at all! Maybe *you'd*
better go in to him," she stormed, which got her nowhere,
not even back to the safety of her own fatigue.

The next morning Joan was sitting in rigid self-defense
beside Alexander, Winifred now righteously upright on his
other side, when Jerry slowed down to examine the high-
way. "There's a side road near here that goes to an old
fortress of some dukes of Burgundy," he said. "Fellow at
the inn last night told me about it. Fact is, it dates back to
the Thirteenth Century, Alex. You might be interested."
Jerry was in a good humor this morning in the perverse way
a bad-tempered person can be when everyone else has become irritable.

Alex, who had been clasping and unclasping his hands
like a pianist kept too long from his instrument, leaned forward, transferring his restlessness to the promise of something new, and they all began watching for the road which
Jerry said should veer to the right. The green hills of the
Côte d'Or country rose to peaks of pale lavender in the distance against a sky intermittently dark with threatening
rain, through which pure golden rays streaked diagonally
across the hills. It was not an ordinary day, and in the tradition of the pathetic fallacy, they believed they would not
find an ordinary place at its end.

Françoise saw it first, a narrow road no wider than the
car, and she cried, "*Voilà! Avancez!*" standing in the car
to thrust her head from the open top as though she were
directing an expedition. But she soon tired, for the road was
long; it took them almost an hour before they came at last
to the foot of a high hill on top of which were the ruins of

an old stone fortress surrounded by a broken yellowed wall, which might also enclose some semblance of a village. There was no sign of life, however, and the thick wall was split open at one place as though tragedy had already crashed through, carrying with it the last of the inhabitants.

At the top of the hill, the road ended in a market square; it was a village after all, but desolate as a crater on the moon. A solitary old woman in wooden shoes and widow's black dress came down the path carrying a pail to the village pump, and she may have seen them or she may not, for she gave no sign; they might have been ghosts from her own past for all the attention she paid to them.

There was an inn, with a terrace on which four fragile metal tables and a dozen chairs stood in the open, but this seemed quite abandoned except for a thin thread of smoke rising from a narrow chimney. In a shed nearby an aged black car was lodged as though it were a museum piece and the other dwellings, certainly uninhabitable, seemed settling into the earth from which their stones had first been taken.

In the market place there were two roads, one winding toward the crest of the village marked by a sign, *Église,* the other curving around a great ruined castle high above their heads, only its tower still intact. They decided to see the castle first and at the end of the road took a foot-path past a dark, damp-smelling dungeon at the castle's base which curved up and around between the old wall and a sheer drop into space below. As the path narrowed, Françoise, third in line, wearing her silly, open-backed French shoes, squealed and caught hold of Alexander's arm; then foolishly she stopped to break off a thread hanging from the hem of her green skirt. When Jerry, behind her, spoke irritably, she released Alexander; but a moment later she turned her ankle at the most hazardous part of the ledge and caught

Alexander's arm and held it stubbornly with her own. This time, Jerry said nothing.

Joan, first in line, felt suddenly cross with Françoise, and began climbing ahead of the others. She had seen that the French girl's dependency and Jerry's sullen jealous look had brought wise mocking comment to Winifred's face (they had scarcely spoken since last night), but Joan did not need her to point out the undeniable appeal of the French girl's authentic beauty in this wild, half-savage place.

Climbing alone into the first bleak, high-walled chamber, roofless to the sky as an eagle's nest on a crag, Joan stood looking up at walls rising forty feet or more from the earth and tried to imagine the past, putting the present from her mind. She refused to hear the others coming near, the French girl's voice birdlike, protesting against the roots along the path, and Winifred, sharp and curious, questioning, "What do you suppose we'd find at the top of that old tower? More weeds—or rats, maybe!" There was silence and then she spoke again. "It's taking our lives in our hands to climb this crazy path!"

Joan quickly retreated from the larger open chamber into a smaller enclosure away from the sound of their voices (of Winifred's voice), and was sitting on a stone seat against a wall when Alexander came in.

"So this is what you found," he said with approval, coming straight over to take her up in his arms. At first he kissed her with a gentle, unhurried pressure, but after a moment he kissed her as though he had been more surprised than she at what there was between them. Then he drew back and looked in her face. "You were waiting for me," he stated, almost in surprise. "Joan—"

"Joan! Joan, where are you?" Even though they drew apart before Winifred charged through the opening, her look was wise and knowing as though she'd seen through stone.

"Fascinating place, isn't it?" she asked, brightly, planting herself before them and staring from one to the other. "Makes you think of funny things, doesn't it?" she challenged in a voice unpleasant enough to destroy any mood.

"The 'funny things' are in your head," Alexander said, staring at her with obvious distaste, but Joan at that moment felt quite cool about Winifred. A brief instant of understanding made her see that Winifred wanted desperately to make some impression, almost any impact without quite knowing how to make the right one; and she was about to say something kind to the woman when she saw that it would not be necessary, for Winifred was reacting to Alexander's irritated response in a most unexpected way.

"In my head," she repeated, but now the anger was gone from her voice, and a seductive undertone had curiously crept in. She even took a few steps closer, passing Joan as though she were no longer there and then laughed, a soft animal laugh low in her throat. "When are you going to know your age, Alexander?" she asked, quite tenderly, putting her hand on his arm.

For an instant, with that strange undercurrent in her words and the new and subtle motion of her hips she had his whole attention and to Joan the whole scene was so astonishing and so unexpected that she stared mesmerized; until she turned her back on both and began hurrying away, stumbling over the rough terrain down the hill through the trees on the sloping path they could have taken up in the first place if they'd looked around.

But a moment later Alexander had caught up with her and put his arm about her shoulders, so together they descended over the dead grass and drew apart only when they had to jump from one boulder to another outside the dungeon door. Then close again, approaching the market square, Alexander gently reproached her for leaving him behind. She did not answer; she could not say that she had seen something frightening in Winifred at that moment and had not wanted to stay.

Not long afterward the woman came down into the square, airy in her manner, and the odd scene above might never have happened. She even spoke to Alexander in a bantering, normal tone of voice to which he did not respond; then briefly, her dark eyes narrowed and her taut chin grew tighter.

Joan thought, perhaps Alexander should check his dislike before it stirs up more dark brew in the woman's mind. They were not halfway through the trip, and some truce among them would have to be made or the rest of this excursion, this lovely wayward journeying into the French past and countryside, would be spoiled.

On the terrace of the inn, a young Frenchwoman stood waiting for them, holding up a heavy key as long as her hand, and she pointed with it to an old yellow stone church on the opposite hill. As they followed her eyes, even the old crone now washing a long white sheet at the pump straightened for a moment to stare as though not even she had seen the church before.

"*La clef de l'église!*" called the young woman, and Jerry, who had been quarreling with Françoise again, came forward and listened as she showed them where to place it under a stone behind the privy when they left. She regretted the inn must be closed until next weekend, she said, but she was paid as guardian only from Friday until Monday; on other days, the village was not visited by tourists nor did the buses come.

The old woman at the pump? someone asked. "*Ah, la*

vieille!" she said, and shrugged. "The very old, they cannot move with the times. For her, alone, one provides—"

Then she pointed out that it looked like rain. It often rained this summer, she said, and perhaps they should not remain here very late; also it would be advisable to shut the top of their car before the rain commenced, which came without much warning, she explained. So Jerry hurried off to the car, which gave his Françoise the chance, with the quick movement of a cat, to take Alexander's arm as though defying the world.

"See that?" whispered Winifred; but Alexander had already patted Françoise's hand and moved away, walking in long strides up the hill toward the *église*.

Single file they followed him over the cobblestoned path from the market place to the small church on the crest. The rolling Burgundian countryside lay far below, its green lush fields and woods dappled with sun but overlaid with shadows of loneliness. The church itself was solid and well-preserved, as though still cared for and loved; its plain belfry and long narrow windows, simple in design, intact, and the warm golden color of the stones and the gradations of light and shadow on its old irregularities had the wisdom of remembered dreams.

It was when they reached the side door of the church that the rain began, a spatter like water from a garden hose, cool and not unpleasant. A moment later, it seemed to burst from the clouds, bringing hailstones bounding at their feet. Jerry came panting up the hill and Françoise seized the iron key from his hand to insert it in the lock. She wasn't strong enough to open the door; even Alexander had to put his shoulder against the hobnailed oak boards before it swung slowly inward upon the dark dry interior.

A smell of damp and rotting earth rose chillingly to their

nostrils, yet they crowded in anyhow like children on an
adventure, laughing and jostling, hurling their voice defiantly up to the old high-beamed ceiling bringing echoes
back eerily above the sound of the pelting rain.

Yet as their eyes grew accustomed to the darkness relieved only by a pale greenish light from the windows, they
grew uneasy, finding this a grimmer and more forsaken
place of worship than they expected. Alexander was the
first to move with any decision; he began lighting matches
which flared briefly to relieve the gloom, and led the way
toward the apse with its crude small altar against a mural
painting at one end. Then suddenly he stooped down and
ran his hand over a great worn slab of stone in the uneven
floor.

"Under these blocks are men, lying dead," he stated, solemnly, and Jerry flashed on his lighter with an oddly brittle
click in the gloom, to show the iron rings in the stones, each
stone large enough to cover a grave, the big rings rusted
but curiously smooth at the center where a hand might
grasp. Françoise, who hated solemnity, dared Jerry to pull
one, dared him gaily, but her voice went too shrill and she
became silent almost as soon as she had spoken.

"I don't like!" she said then, with an exaggerated shudder, and danced away toward the altar, the focal point of
that vast Christian cavern. Then she screamed, *"Mon
Dieu!"* and hastily crossed herself as they all came and stood
in sudden silence before the flaking murals of emaciated
corpses rising from the dead, climbing out of coffins and
graves in a vast macabre landscape that covered the altar
wall.

The figures seemed distressingly human with sickly gray
skin, open mouths and hollow eyes, struggling up each from
some unimagined Hell, perhaps called by the Saviour—but
where was He? The central emaciated figure was still

trapped in the gaping wound of the grave, and it was this
creature that held them uneasily silent; some strange pig-
mentation, perhaps of human blood, gave livid shadows to
the stretched tendons of the arms and legs as clawed hands
reached agonizingly for help to the figures risen ahead of
him—but in the aperture, or grave, his own lower limbs
were trapped, forever now, in flames.

The little group of the living drew together, except for
Winifred who alone seemed unimpressed, disdainful. She
stood near a window where the tinted glass cast a greenish
light over her long Protestant nose and forehead, reflectively looking out on the lessening rain, the day, where the
sun was beginning to flicker through. She had cast scarcely
a glance at the murals, and finally they all turned away to
move uneasily about the church, to see what little else there
was and then to leave. Alexander found a decaying organ
in a distant corner, but as his trained hands touched the
keys, no music sounded; only a hollow breath came out like
a balloon emptying of air. His face became sad then, as
though memory had betrayed him, and Joan put out her
hand. She understood now what she could do, and if the
others had not been there, she would have put her arms
around him.

But at that moment Françoise clattered over the bare floor
with her pointed heels and rushed out into the light, with a
little shriek. The moment broken, Joan followed, relieved to
find that outdoors the world was once more miraculously
green and blue and almost sunny: she was glad to leave the
uncomfortable church behind. Françoise stooped and picked
up hailstones caught in the hollows of the ground which
she thrust at Jerry when he followed her; and he tossed
these into the valley below, over the cliff and trees, then
both gathered all they could find, flinging the bright bau-
bles wildly in the air. To Joan the game seemed an absurdly

happy one and when Françoise ran back inside the church calling "Aleex! Aleex, come play!" she stooped and gathered hailstones herself to throw at Alex when he would appear.

As Françoise vanished inside the church, she brushed past Winifred who stood, almost pensively, in the doorway, with a curious smile on her face; but no one could possibly have been prepared the next moment for the crazy thing they saw her do. . . .

She seized the heavy oak door by its iron handle, stepped back outside and pulled it shut quickly, hard; then she turned the great key in the lock and stood there mocking them all.

"What the hell!" exclaimed Jerry, turning sharply from his game, for now Alex and his Françoise were locked together inside the church—anyone would know, Joan thought, that Jerry would be angry. And indeed he came tearing back toward Winifred to thrust her violently away from the door, snatching the key from her hand. Yet it was not until he tried to turn the key in the lock and failed, when the old door held fast as though it never would be opened again, that Joan realized the terrible thing that Winifred had done. Even when finally Jerry did get the rusty key to turn the door itself held, stubborn and hard, as though having submitted to man's will for so many centuries, now nothing less than a miracle would open it again.

"Let me in!" Jerry shouted, leaning hard against the door. "Françoise, pull, for Christ's sake! Alex, open the door, damn it—*pull!*"

But the door would not budge. No matter how Jerry pushed or anyone else pulled, even though Alex rattled the ring from inside and obviously strained as they were straining—they could hear him breathing and swearing too— there was no way to budge the heavy barrier between them.

The man and woman inside were trapped as surely, Joan thought in sudden terror, as in a tomb!

At last Winifred looked frightened and began to push on the door, protesting she had not known they were still inside, had she? That she was sure everyone had come out before she'd closed the door, so they couldn't blame her. It was a natural mistake, she insisted, becoming quite as distraught as if she had been innocent.

Joan then ran around in front of the church, remembering the door there but this was locked like the other, and held as fast; she came hurrying back, concerned for Jerry who looked frightened and now exhausted, breathing hard and unnaturally as he rested for a moment on the ground. In the silence sudden thunder startled them and Jerry leaped again to his feet.

"Françoise!" he cried, his ear straining against the door. "Baby! Baby, answer me—are you all right in there? For Christ's sake—"

Unexpectedly at this moment they heard Françoise giggle. With some relief they even listened as the girl's light soprano came trilling a few words from a French song about *"mon amour."* She interrupted herself to call, "It is a joke, now I know! We stay here, and you make the joke—well, we are having a fine time, Aleex *et moi!* Ah, you will be jealous when you know!"

It was better, of course, that she was not alarmed, thought Joan, as Jerry swore violently and struggled hard; if the door had opened once, surely it must open again. But poor Jerry was nearly beside himself as, bending over, his hands on his knees, he strained and shoved at the door with his bulletlike head and all the muscles of his broad young back were bulged and sweating.

Perhaps the young woman at the inn, Joan thought, can tell us what to do. She may not have left; perhaps there is another key. So she ran down the hill toward the pump, where the old woman straightened as Joan ran up but then turned again to her slow, absorbing task just as Joan saw with a shock that the black car from the inn was even then moving off down the road in the distance. And as she watched, it vanished behind a border of trees, so now there was no one left in the deserted village but the senile old woman endlessly at her wash.

In halting French Joan tried to explain what had happened. Was there anyone who could help? Was there another key? The old creature stared from yellow squinting eyes, exposing toothless gums, then she laughed soundlessly as though she found them all insane. . . .

Back at the church Jerry was sitting on the ground with his head in his hands and groaning, whether from despair or injury Joan did not know. Winifred was hugging her light sweater about herself, walking nervously from one spot to another, and Françoise was calling from inside that she thought the joke had gone far enough, even though she was having fun with Aleex.

"*Très, très amusant, M'sieu Crowell,*" she volunteered, and went off in a peal of laughter close to hysteria. Alexander yelled, "When in God's name are you going to get us out of this mausoleum?—You're still trying, aren't you, out there?"

They heard Françoise laugh and tell him not to be silly, not to "worrie," of course Jerry would not go one step without her.

"Jerrie!" she screamed suddenly, and this time they knew it was not Alexander pounding on the door.

The young husband got up and threw himself at the heavy barrier, and finally, suddenly, it gave way. Sprawling, he fell in upon the stone floor almost at the feet of Françoise who had one hand pressed tight against her mouth and her eyes squeezed shut. Then she began to cry, bending over Jerry and cradling him in her arms until angrily he scrambled to his feet, pulling her outside.

"What the hell did she do a thing like that for?" Alexander demanded of Joan as he came out blinking into the bright sunny day, staring at Winifred with almost threatening hostility. "You shut that door on purpose, by God!"

Winifred's face remained taut and closed as Alexander set off angrily down the hill, his feet slapping hard on the old, round stones.

"Look at him," she whispered to Joan, as though they were fellow conspirators. "Now you see what I mean. *They* weren't the ones upset, they didn't care about being locked in there with all those naked pictures. Oh, no. We were the ones driven half crazy!"

In place of her recent and transient look of guilt and fear, something quite different had now come into Winifred's face, something crazed and cunning. Joan stared with a rising sense of alarm, then she, too, fled down the hill, catching up with Alexander who did not pause in his headlong stride until he'd reached the car and got into the back seat, drawing Joan in with him.

The others came down a moment later, but he did not move apart from Joan, even when Winifred stood staring in on them. "Well," she said brightly, "you seem pretty nicely settled, you two. What a day!" And she laughed as though she'd been right about something, all along. She would have climbed in the front seat then, but Françoise pushed past her and got in first, twisting her knees to cover all the space, and Jerry got in from the other side, his young jaw tense and red with anger.

"Well, make up your minds, where do I sit?" asked Winifred with mock good humor. But when the four faces looked out and no one moved, a certain uneasiness appeared in her eyes.

Over by the pump the old woman had paused in her washing and was looking, too, interested at last in these odd creatures from the outer world.

"You sit—" Jerry made a vulgar sound, at which his wife clapped her hand over her mouth with a shrill explosion of laughter. "No room here, ma'am," he went on. "Sorry—full up."

"They're joking," Winifred said, appealing to Joan, her thin hand reaching out, gripping the front door. "We should be getting on, too— Why, we'll have to be finding a place for the night, we're all starved. That's why we're so upset! Look, it was my fault, Jerry, so dinner will be on me. Wherever you want to stop—you pick the place and I'll pay the bill."

How childish, thought Joan, seeing Winifred's eyes flare out over the deserted square as she held fast to the car door with her tense right hand. The old woman had vanished at last and the sky was darkening again. Far below, the fields were cut in squares and oblongs and triangles like pasted cutouts, but there were no houses anywhere, and there had been no one on the narrow road except the woman driver of the old black car for a long, long time.

Françoise also followed Winifred's eyes in their brief survey. "Take a bus!" she cried, suddenly screaming with laughter, and tugged on Jerry's arm for his approval.

"It was a mistake, you must believe that," Winifred pleaded. "And even so—" she went on reasonably, "how could I know the door would stick? It worked all right when we first went in." They all saw her left hand tremble as she pushed back a strand of hair from her eyes to see them better, and Joan thought, It won't do—someone has to give in. The rain had started again, lightly but pattering steadily on the roof of the car, without fanfare this time, so one knew it would last. It was time they drove on, found a place to stay for the night, as Winifred had said—but she was not prepared for what happened then, nor was anyone.

For suddenly the car shot away—Jerry must have pressed hard on the accelerator—throwing the passengers against their seats in unexpected confusion. It was not until a moment later that they looked back and saw Winifred in the rain holding up a white hand as though it had been injured, the fingers bent; crying, she was starting to run after them.

"Turn back, Jerry!" Alexander sharply demanded, leaning over the front seat as though he would take the wheel from the angry young man. "Don't be a fool. You can't leave the woman alone in a place like that!"

"I can't, can't I?" And the car careened around the square under Jerry's taut determined hands.

Even Françoise was silenced as Jerry raced out of the deserted village and down the hill twenty times faster than they had climbed it, following the abandoned road and finally swerving dangerously over the narrow bridge at the turn, skidding out gravel across the grassy ditch into the valley.

He did not stop, even though they all kept saying he must, and after awhile Françoise began singing her French song about love in a sweetly plaintive voice as the rain beat down harder than ever upon the roof which sheltered them.

The Truth About
a Frenchman

When the No. 85 bus stopped, Nancy Greenhill jumped off at the rue d'Assas and ran back to the entrance of 22 rue Madame. Racing across the inner courtyard, with its spindly bushes and single brave flowering shrub, she climbed the curving stairs of the pension with just four minutes to spare before luncheon. Already there was a small cluster of the professors' wives waiting, their shoulders back and hands clasped in studied repose, for the moment Simone's bell would ring. Today even old Mme du Coeur, who rarely was well enough to make an appearance, waited too, her fragile, arthritic hands clutching the arms of her wheelchair.

Anticipating their resentment, Nancy still dared interrupt this little tableau by asking Simone if there had been any calls for her. Simone, holding her brass dinner bell poised for a quick downward swing at the stroke of twelve-thirty, said *"Rien!"* and flashed a triumphant look at the American girl so obviously forgotten by her lover.

At this moment Mme Lévy, the elderly American expa-

triate who had once met James Joyce in the bookshop of
Sylvia Beach, and whose stomach rumblings they heard
every day minutes before the bell was rung, began to hold
forth on Frenchmen, her favorite topic for conversation.

"If you want to know the truth about a Frenchman,"
Mme Lévy stated as one whose knowledge and experience
on this subject were *sans pareil,* "it's something you learn
the hard way, if you're ever fool enough to marry one of
the rascals." Unable to raise even a flicker of interest among
the professors' wives, she turned with a hopeful, if inquisi-
tive glance toward Nancy. "And you, girl, is that what
you're here for? Looking for a French husband?"

Fortunately, the clock struck the half-hour and Simone
clanged her bell with the spirit of a virtuoso: no answer
was needed. They all surged into the dining salon and rapidly took their accustomed places at the two long tables
spread like duplicate stage settings under spotlighting rays
from the sun, the small wooden napkin rings and half-
emptied wine bottles marking each neat place setting. Mme
Lévy's chair was four places away from Nancy's, and generally the old woman's voracious curiosity could be distracted
by an equally voracious appetite; but it wasn't at all hard
for the girl to imagine that if Mme Lévy were persistent
enough, she could find out that Nancy *had* come here for
a French husband—even one who was not her own.

On the other hand, it was conceivable that Mme Lévy, if
given half a chance, just might have valuable information
on the French male character, a subject at the moment
deeply troubling the American girl. Why had not Pierre,
after so many tender allusions to the past in his letters,
called her in three days? Why had he not acknowledged the
pneumatique that she'd sent when she arrived in Paris
Wednesday night? Would it be wise, strategically, for a girl

to telephone him, since for so long he had been urging her to come?

But now the old woman, apparently deciding that Nancy was as indifferent to clever conversation as the professors' wives, was ignoring everyone, her boney old profile bent near-sightedly but hungrily over her plate. And even after the girl leaned forward to ask, "What *is* the truth about the Frenchman, Mme Lévy?" for a moment, she maintained a frigid silence.

Then slowly she turned her hooded gaze. "Oh, now you want to know," she chided, but one could see she was appeased, as she rested her wise and cynical eyes almost sympathetically on the girl's seemingly candid face. "They tell me at my age I should talk less and listen more, if I know what's good for me," she stated insincerely. "Why should any young woman of today care what *une vieille guenon* might have learned through half a century's passionate study of *l'art de l'amour?*"

"Mme Lévy, tell us about *l'art de l'amour*," the young Englishman urged, laughingly, before Nancy had to speak. In fact, all faces were turned toward Mme Lévy now, and even the professors' wives stopped nibbling on their bread to exchange amused glances over Nancy's head. "Come now, Mme Lévy, tell us the truth about love and the jolly Frenchmen, do!" teased the English boy.

Naturally, then, Mme Lévy sat up straight as an actress who has found at last the audience she deserves. "The truth?" she scoffed, with a flirtatious toss of her head. "It's always the truth you want, you young." Then for a moment she seemed oddly to falter, or rather to have to search further back than one would have thought necessary among the sophistries in her mind. At last, however, she gave a most oracular nod. "The truth," she said, "is that no woman can live with one of those French rascals—she can only live for him—and for his mistresses!"

Oh, nonsense, thought Nancy, who'd almost begun to believe that the old woman might reveal something worthwhile.

"Nonsense!" came unexpectedly from old Mme du Coeur at the head of the table. "You speak always as an American, Mme Lévy. Your judgments are naïve. As a Frenchwoman, I must challenge this absurd declaration!"

To everyone's surprise Mme Lévy subsided then, abashed as a young girl who, after forty years, has not yet recovered from her fear of a tyrannical French mother-in-law.

"The only truth *I* know about Frenchmen is that they put up this wall," complained a stout, homely American girl who was a summer student at the University. "Just when you think you're getting somewhere, they either get too fresh, or they put up this barrier. I didn't expect anything like that when I came to Paris."

"The truth, Mme Lévy, is," continued old Mme du Coeur, ignoring the interruption, "only a Frenchwoman can understand a *Frenchman!*"

It was at this moment that the telephone in the hall pealed out sharply, dramatically, for all to hear.

" 'Allo, 'allo," came Simone's voice. *"Ne quittez pas!"* And she came hurrying in with a congratulatory smile, "It is a gentleman for Mme Greenhill!"

Knowing the two old women's eyes were upon her, Nancy tried not to get up hastily; but in the hall once she'd put the two receivers of the old fashioned French phone to her ears, she could not be calm. "Hello—Pierre?" she sang out even before she heard his voice.

"Ah, Nancy, it is I. How go things with you—after these long years?"

"Wonderful, now. Oh, Pierre—"

"Perhaps you think I do not remember to call. You are not angry that I am not telephoning before?"

"Oh, no." She tried to speak more sensibly now, not because others might be listening, but because Pierre was very cool, himself. "I've been getting acclimated—you know, re-visiting the scenes of my youth." Even after ten years, the sound of his deep shaded voice could upset the delicate equilibrium of her senses. How could she ever have married Tex?—"It's good to hear your voice," she said, quickly, but more soberly.

"Your voice is also agreeable," he said politely. Then there was a brief pause as he spoke to someone behind him. "I am in my office," he explained. "Unfortunately—So, did you have a good journey? Are you well content there on *la rive gauche?*" As with most well-bred Frenchmen, he spoke of the Left Bank with amusement; this was a part of Paris one had visited in one's student days, but seldom thereafter.

"Oh, yes—I am *content.*" She said with only slightly less confidence.

"Good. *Alors*—are you free to meet me for the cocktails at the Café Colisée on the Champs Élysées? *À cinq heures et demi.*" Then, briefly, he relaxed into an old and familiar lightness. "So that you know me still, I am wearing a blue necktie. With fishtails, red and white fishtails."

"A blue necktie with red and white fishtails," she repeated. "Red, white and blue, like the American flag," she joked.

"*Mais non!* Frenchmen wear their own colors now," he corrected her. "We meet then—together?"

"At *cinq heures et demi,*" she agreed, quickly.

"And we must speak English. You must give me practice again in my *vocabulaire,*" he said, almost tenderly.

"I've forgotten most of my French. . . . Pierre, you did

want me to come back, didn't you?" She could not hold this in any longer, but the brief silence which followed was not quite reassuring. Then his voice came, quite soberly, even a little sad.

"Of course, it is a joy that you are in Paris. But—you must be prepared for some change. Much water—*comment dit-on?*—goes over the bridge in these years. Perhaps I will not be quite as you expect?"

"I'm prepared for anything," she said rashly, believing this was true.

"Then, *chérie, au revoir*," he said, the old loving note she remembered quite clear in his voice.

"*Au revoir, Pierre*," she said, her lips held close to the cold mouthpiece.

When she returned to the table everyone smilingly stared so it was apparent Mme Lévy had been talking again. "Now, I would say that call was from a Frenchman," she said, tipping her dyed brown head impishly to one side. "Only one of those rascals could bring such a look of delight and confusion and expectation all at the same time to the face of an American girl."

Mme du Coeur said, "Humph!"

"Do they do that?" asked the American girl student, hopefully. Then despairingly, she shook her head. "It's just that when you least expect it, the wall is *there*," she said.

Dressing that afternoon, Nancy thought how she had met Pierre at the end of her year at school in Lausanne where she'd been enlightened about European men by girls from twenty-nine countries. Already she had begun to anticipate their Gallic ways, so different from boys she had known before; so it had seemed like fate when Pierre appeared at an Embassy party more handsome, and more flattering than anyone else in the company. Almost at once he'd complimented her on her French accent. It was more natural than most American's, he'd said.

"That is because I have become French in my thinking," she had claimed, airily, but Pierre's dark eyes had stared back in alarm and disbelief.

"What is this you say?" he had asked loudly there on the crowded, green Embassy lawn. "That you are French in your thinking, when you are American?"

She had learned quite a few tricks from the European girls, and one was to let her face become feminine and acquiescent when faced with someone's disapproval. "That *is* presumptive, of course," she'd agreed, sweetly. "I was only speaking wishfully, I guess."

He had not let it go at that, however, for this was the time of the Algerian war. "Do you then have nightmares of fighting a war you hate, of attacking your brother whom you must kill, of not then knowing the reason why? Tell me, Mademoiselle American, if you think like the French, how would *you* end our Algerian war?"

She'd stared at him miserably, seeing how serious he was, and she began to love him at that moment. Then he'd forgiven her and taken her away from the Embassy and after that they had been so close—but a month later the Algerian war had taken *him,* and it seemed that all was ended.

Maybe it was because she wore a white dress and fresh white gloves and her eyes and lips glistened in anticipation, that the waiter gave her a very choice table on the terrace of the Café Colisée. And when Pierre came along, carrying a cane with the air of a true boulevardier, the waiter almost seemed to speak his pride in having judged his clientèle correctly.

Pierre had a full dark English mustache now, and as he walked more slowly she had time to glance at her reflection in the window of the café behind, wondering if she still looked as he would remember her. They always had looked well together, he with his saturnine, Parisian face, she with her healthy curving look of the American Anglo-Saxon; but now it seemed he had grown beyond her in years and sophistication in some exciting but disturbing way; and then she noticed his limp.

He did not greet her until he had settled rather awkwardly at the table, his silver-headed cane between well-pressed knees, one of which remained unbending. Then he turned almost at once to examine pretty girls around them, a gesture which puzzled her, since it was obviously an act of self-consciousness. Finally he looked at her.

"So Nancy, you have come back," he stated, a challenging note in his voice. "You have come back to Paris. Why?" he asked, coolly.

"Why?" Back home she had imagined this moment, how she would say she'd kept thinking, all these years, how they never had a chance to say good-bye. How one night they were together (yes, together!) and the next, he was gone. "Well, in your letters," she began, and faltered. "I thought you wanted to see me. And—. We never really had a chance to say good-bye," she added, bravely.

"So you have come back now to say good-bye?" This seemed to amuse him. "It is such a sentimental reason, *chérie!*"

"Yes, isn't it?" For a moment she stiffened defensively. "But some sentiments are natural, I should think," she said.

"Ah, yes." He looked at her more kindly now. "If one can forget that it is sentiment which brings about wars and nationalism—so many foolish things." He shifted his left leg and caught her looking at it. "No, after Algiers I do not ski as before," he said. "Did we ever ski together?—I do not remember."

"I never knew you in winter," she said. Perhaps it was because of this injury he married his cousin, she thought suddenly. "We went swimming in the piscine in the Seine, and we played tennis in the Bois. And we walked and walked under the chestnut trees," she ended, appealing to him to look at her now, to break down the barrier.

"All that is ended," he said flatly, staring with exaggerated attentiveness at a flirting girl two tables away. "It is fortunate my wife is not an athlete, is it not? If we had married, you and I," he went on briskly, "it would have been so boring for you when I cannot do these things you Americans like so much."

"I've done those things—and I've still been bored," she said; and then, he responded. His eyes became dark as though he were suddenly intensely aware of her, and for a moment he leaned forward. "Can it be that you are the same, Nancy? And I think you are more beautiful than before!" But he changed again. "American women are like that, I think. You do not change." Now almost angrily he took up the wine card, which he at once tossed aside to order a martini. Then he offered her an American cigarette, shifted his left leg with a tensing of chin muscles and said, "Surely, Nancy, you cannot believe you are the same in love with me? What of this husband in your United States?"

"He tries to understand," she said, avoiding his first question. But as Pierre continued to stare she said, quietly. "By your letters, you seemed to feel the same about me." She met his eyes almost in defiance.

"Yes, well, so." He spoke noncommittally, then he took up his cane, examined its silver head and placed it upright beside his bad leg. "I tell Claire," he said unexpectedly. "I tell her that an old friend—a very *good* old friend—is in Paris." He looked at his wristwatch. "So—Claire asks will you dine with us, *chez nous*, one evening during the next fortnight?"

"You *told* her?"

A look of amusement came into Pierre's eyes. "I have not tell her everything," he said, almost teasingly, but she could not smile. Instead, very stiffly, she said, "I may leave Paris too soon for that. I have never been to Florence, and now I have the time, I may go. I have friends who want me to come."

Surprisingly this seemed to upset him. "But you have only just arrived!" he exclaimed, and quite as though they were not in a public café he took her hand and pressed his crisp mustache and warm lips against her palm. "I think you are not understanding, Nancy. What I try to say . . . You must not leave now!" He spoke as though he really did care. "But you must understand, *chérie*, how in France these days no man is quite free. Life is more serious—This does not mean I do not love you!"

She stared at him, afraid to trust speech with her lips quivering: this was how she'd known it would be from the start. This was why she had come. "How could I leave now?" she asked, and tried to laugh because she felt suddenly so terribly vulnerable.

When they parted soon after, the remote smile had returned to Pierre's handsome face, and some of the skepticism; but by then Nancy had her answer to the question in her mind. Pierre did want her still, and she had been right to come.

"How was the French *apéritif?*" asked the incorrigible old Mme Lévy at dinner that night. "Or did you have a *fine champagne?* One is served before a good meal and the other usually comes after," she explained to the young Englishman who joined her in knowing laughter. Then she wagged a long admonishing finger at Nancy. "An American girl had better stick to martinis, if she has any idea what's best for her. That's the best and safest drink in any country. It cools the blood rather than burns it."

"Gin doesn't agree with me," said Nancy, defiantly. "My favorite drink is champagne. French champagne." As she expected, however, on the stairs after dinner, Madame was waiting.

"I had a French husband, child," she said. "A veritable rabbit with women—although it was my father-in-law who was most truly French. He gave his wife anything he gave his mistress. That way, who could complain? Once it was a sable coat worth a fortune—" Shrewdly she peered in Nancy's face. "How would you, a spoiled American girl, like to be one of a pair?" she asked.

"I doubt if a fur coat would seem that important these days," Nancy responded, coldly. "Wasn't that a very long time ago, Mme Lévy?"

"Frenchmen don't change," said the old woman, the light on the landing coming down like a beacon on her pinched, aristocratic nose. "They're clever as foxes in keeping women bound to them. I advise you, girl, go home on the next plane!"

Nancy's proper answer was that what she did concerned no one but herself, but remembering how cautious Pierre had been, the old woman's warning seemed funny and a little sad. It was only in her room with the door closed that a kind of depression settled over her, so that she wrote a letter to Tex just to say where she was staying and how things were at the pension. And she wanted him to know she hadn't forgotten how nice he'd been about everything. She really did wish things had worked out differently.

When three days went by without any word from Pierre,

Nancy was glad she'd written home. A letter came from Tex, crossing hers in mid-ocean, and she thought how hard it had been to tell him the truth about coming back to France. "That's a great idea, Nancy," he'd exclaimed when first she said she wanted to go. "We'll make it a second honeymoon!"

There had been no way out then but to explain how that was not what she had in mind. Tex, who already knew about Pierre, listened without expression as she said that Pierre had been writing again, that he was not happy in his life and that she'd been so upset by his letters that she knew she hadn't gotten over him. "But I don't want to hurt you, Tex," she'd said.

"Why should you?" he'd asked, reasonably, his big blond head turned to listen carefully.

"Well, maybe I never stopped being in love with him—"

"In that case," he said quietly, "I guess that eliminates me."

She'd tried to tell him how awful she felt about everything, but that she couldn't honestly go on—not, at least, until she found out how she really felt. She said this to make him feel better, but she thought she knew: it was still Pierre she loved.

"Oh, I'll get over it," Tex had said, not nastily, but a little cold. "The guy may have changed more than you think, though—"

"Maybe," she'd conceded, since she'd not shown him the letters. If she had, he'd know as well as she did how Pierre felt.

Tex's letter was casual, saying he'd written because her father was nagging him about her. Then he went on about how he'd crossed from Westport to Port Jefferson in a cabin cruiser, staying for a weekend with their mutual friends, the Potters (Madeline sent her love), where the

Bloody Marys were big as buckets. It was when she began to think how good a cold big Bloody Mary could be that Nancy telephoned Pierre.

He did not seem surprised and earnestly explained that his wife had been busy with the wedding of her niece; but that Claire had made him promise, next time he talked to Nancy, to invite her home for dinner.

It took a moment for Nancy to answer. "I called about lunch today," she said. "In return for the drinks. Just you and me," she said, stubbornly.

"Oh, perhaps—" He turned from the telephone and she could hear him consulting his secretary. "Unfortunately, today I have a client from Germany for lunch," he said. "I am so sorry."

"Tomorrow, then," she persisted. "I may not stay here much longer."

"Tomorrow," he agreed quickly. "Then we will plan for you and Claire to meet."

Feeling quite angry, Nancy hurried past Simone skating on her floor-polishing brushes, and went into her room where she opened her mail. Her father had written that he hoped she was getting this French bug out of her system, that it had been a mistake to send her abroad in the first place when she'd been such an impressionable kid; and that she'd better know that Tex was going around a lot with a pretty girl from Long Island.

She and Pierre met at the Café de Paris on the avenue de l'Opéra, which with traffic being as it was, was not at all intimate, but still very far from her father and Tex's world at home. At least, Nancy thought, sipping her white wine, a Meursault of '59 was to be preferred to a martini, in an atmosphere like Paris.

Nothing pleased Pierre more than to have one rely on his

judgment in food and drink, and he made a ritual of choos-
ing, solemnly, dishes he thought she would like best after
her long dull diet of American food. Then he made fun of
the bad French spoken by some Americans at the next
table, and said he had never known a woman to look so
well-dressed as Nancy, without a hat. She'd had to push
down a small sense of guilt when she observed that one of
the ladies at the next table looked like Tex's mother, whom
she liked, and refused to be embarrassed by that. The wind
had left her hair in a mess. But there was no intimacy between them until, again, just before they separated. Then
Pierre took her hand under the table, looked with loving
intensity into her eyes and said that it was ridiculous to
think he could live another day without her.

After he left in his taxi—she had said she would go to
the American Express in the neighborhood—she walked to
the rue St.-Honoré and bought a big important hat right
out of the window; and that night she went dancing with
an American pilot and, with him, made fun of some French
couple quarreling loudly at the next table. It was an amusing evening, but in the dream she had later she and Pierre
and Tex were all three chasing one another down the
Champs Élysées, she after Pierre, and Tex after both of
them, and the distances got wider and wider the longer she
stayed asleep.

Pierre called next day, and they met for drinks near his
office on the rue de Berri. He said he had been thinking,
that while their feelings were precious, well, the world had
changed, and he would not know what to offer her now if
she remained in Paris. A Frenchman did not have money
these days for the cost of the worthwhile things in life, since
De Gaulle dictated everything they must do (this he passed
off with only a hint of bitterness) ; also, he said with a small

laugh, French wives were not as ignorant of finances as their *grand'mères* had been.

Nancy started to cry and agreed he was probably right, and said she would leave right away. This so upset him he said she was misunderstanding him again, that he only wanted her to be prepared, that, well, some things would have to depend on her. Did she understand?

No, she did not understand, so he took her in his racing car and drove into the Bois de Boulogne, saying he would explain. But when they came to an abandoned playground he stopped the car and kissed her, saying all that truly mattered was that they had found each other again, and she must have faith that everything could be arranged. Nancy could not help but respond with her senses; yet when he drove her back across Paris, holding her hand tight on his knee, he could barely take time to jump out and open the door for her before he shot away again, saying Claire would be getting impatient waiting dinner on the rue Chalgrin.

When she entered the dining room, late, everyone turned and stared, and Mme Lévy said to Mme du Coeur: "In my day, a Frenchman kept to one rule at least, no matter what deviltry he might be up to; he always brought a lady back at the proper hour for dinner!" The other old woman haughtily agreed.

For two more days Pierre did not call, nor did Nancy receive more letters from home. She spent hours walking the streets of Paris, telling herself that she had taken too much for granted all her life. Then Pierre called again.

He called, he said, because Claire was disconsolate that she had not met his good American friend; and so, could Nancy dine with them, this evening?

Nancy took a long, brave breath and said, well, yes, tonight she was free—for a change. He said he would report to Claire, and five minutes later, for the first time as prompt as he had said he would be, announced that Claire was delighted. At seven then, he would call for Nancy and they would drive to the rue Chalgrin where Claire would joyfully receive them.

Nancy dressed very carefully in the patterned silk she'd been saving for an occasion, and wore her small mink cape (she wondered if she should inform Mme Lévy her father had bought this for her!). As Pierre came in through the dark archway, his black hair gleaming and his limp only slightly apparent, she looked back up at the windows, and there, sure enough, were Mme Lévy and the professors' wives looking down at her as though whatever she was about to do could be the subject of delighted conversation for all the rest of their evening.

Pierre drove very fast through the narrow streets until he reached the broad Champs de Mars. Only then did he turn to look at her. "That is the perfect dress for this evening," he said, approvingly. "Claire will like that. She will consider it very chic." This so annoyed Nancy that for a moment she thought it might have been more comfortable to keep on pretending his wife had never existed.

"You aren't nervous, are you?" he asked, suddenly.

"Good heavens, I don't think so." Then she thought for a moment and realized, annoyingly, that she was. "But it's not the most natural thing in the world, is it?" she asked.

"It is amusing," he said. "And I must tell you that Claire is also nervous. She has telephoned three times this afternoon, to ask what she should wear! Also if you would prefer *oeufs en gelée* to *pâté de foie gras,* and if you like best the Scotch or the gin."

"Oh," said Nancy, faintly. "Isn't she going to a lot of trouble?"

"But of course," said Pierre, cheerfully. "I tell her this she must do." They had stopped briefly for the heavy traffic congested around the Étoile, and swiftly he took her hand, raising it to his cool cheeks and then to his lips. "My brave Nancy," he said. "Everything will be hokay—you will see. You will understand many things after tonight, *ma chérie*."

Understand, perhaps, but she was not sure she would be more easy in her mind. For when the French wife flung open the doors of a beautiful modern apartment, Nancy was quite unprepared for Claire's extreme youth, and her attractiveness. She looked no more than twenty, with light brown hair and a wide, smiling mouth in which perfect teeth seemed childishly white and strong; and her body, in a Givenchy dress, was supple and narrow as a mannequin's, the very short skirt flaring above beautiful, thin, little-girl knees. This was not the image of the cousin Nancy had imagined for Pierre.

"How do you do?" said Claire, in stilted, schoolgirl English.

"I tell you, Nancy speak very good French," said Pierre, almost irritably. Then almost tenderly, "It is a long time ago, but Nancy does not forget what I have teach her."

The marvelous thing was that Claire became even more friendly then, like a playful kitten: *adorable,* Nancy decided was the word, feeling somewhat disconcerted. And when Claire served a splendid dinner with the help of a nervous young maid, Nancy was not surprised to see more than once the smiling, almost paternal approval on Pierre's handsome face—although he had not been pleased with the martinis, which she'd made with sweet Vermouth. However, the Bordeaux she served with the gigot was excellent, he said, and forgave her.

Sitting in the stylish room after dinner, a room that might have been in the apartment of any young couple in

New York, Claire said, contentedly, "Now we are three friends." Curling her long thin legs under her on the brown modern sofa, she went on disarmingly: "Always Pierre, he talk and talk about his Nancy, his *old* friend." If the girl were not smiling so warmly Nancy might have wondered if she emphasized the difference in their ages, but Claire's eyes were too smiling for that. "Pierre say, when the babies come we name one Nancy. Although to be sure, our babies will be boys." She smiled enchantingly. "When a wife is very much loving, the boy babies come first, my grand'mère says."

Pierre, for once, cast a startled look at his wife, just as the fine French clock on the mantel struck ten. Hastily, Nancy got to her feet: surely it was late enough to go. The evening, after all, had been a strain and she felt oddly depressed. She could not imagine now why Pierre had been so anxious for her and Claire to meet.

"You have been so kind," she said to Claire.

"Ah, but you are kind," said the girl as Pierre stood looking from one to the other with a gaze of almost equal pride. Yet his dark eyes were mocking, as though he were amused too, by something neither of them had yet guessed.

"I will drive Nancy to the pension," he said with appropriate courtesy, but Claire, to Nancy's surprise, objected. "It is too late, Pierre," she said, quite sharply. "A taxi go much more fast. You must not go again tonight, because you work early in the morning."

"Oh of course not, I'll take a cab," said Nancy quickly, not wanting a small gallantry of Pierre's to spoil the precarious balance of the evening.

Pierre, rather irritably, went limping off down the stairs to find a taxi for Nancy, leaving them together. Claire, Nancy saw uncomfortably, was staring with her big, drooping, gray-green eyes. "You finish here? You go home now?"

"Yes," said Nancy, arrested by the unexpected antagonism in the girl's voice. "Soon, yes, I think—"

"*Bien!*" said Claire, ignoring Nancy's hand held out in good-bye. "You Americans, you are too rich and clever for our Frenchmen." Then, her eyes narrowing but with an air light as a feather, she added, "You Americans—it is better, you go home!"

Nancy, in dismay, observed that now the girl's face was plain and cross as a tempestuous child's. But the French girl only tossed her head and looked away, and it was then she said the significant thing. "I read these letters you write to Pierre. He tell me everything, you understand? He show me his letters, too." She turned back and stared triumphantly at Nancy. "He say—he write to you for the one reason: for the practice in his English *vocabulaire!*"

Nancy could not remember later what she'd said, but it seemed she'd murmured something and then hurried out the door. The stair light was cut off before she reached the bottom of the stairs, so she had to grope her way out where Pierre was waiting like a lover to draw her into the shadows.

"Ah, *chérie,*" he whispered. "Now you see. Now you understand how your Pierre has suffered for so long?"

"No," she said, resisting. "No, Pierre, I don't see . . ."

"You do not see how Claire think you have come to take me away? How she will lose me? It is pathological! Ah, but tonight, *chérie,* with the little plot, we show her all is well. Now, she has no more fear!" Then he added excitedly, "Now you must find the little apartment. Like this, only more small, not so expensive. Something for—a thousand francs? Yes, I think for a thousand francs—or a little more —you find something, desirable—that is not too much, is it? . . . Then we can be together on certain days—and nights, *chérie!* Claire will think you return to America and so she too will be content. How clever you are!" he said as

Claire had said earlier, and then his lips roamed over her face, his body pressed demandingly against hers.

"Pierre, stop—no, listen," she said, for she could not help stiffening and she did not want to be kissed now. She did not want to be kissed at any moment here in the dark beneath Claire's window. "I'm not clever. It's Claire who is the clever one, Pierre—She *knows*, Pierre."

He put back his head and laughed, then brought her against him again. "Foolish Nancy," he murmured against her neck. "What can Claire know that I do not tell her? She is only a child, a little girl. While you, my darling, you are a woman, strong, mature—*you* know how to live life, to love—"

Tenderly he kissed her eyes, and then, deep and meaningfully, her mouth. And for a moment there was no wall between them, and wasn't this what she had come to find? She even tried to respond, to return the pressure of his body with hers. . . .

"Pierre!" The voice came shrilly from above their heads after a window was suddenly flung open. "Pierre, where are you?"

Laughing, Pierre pushed Nancy back into the shadows and they both listened as the maid came and spoke to Claire, to Claire's voice in reply, scolding about the *flageolet*, a *catastrophe*. And surely the stupid girl had been told often enough about the temperature of the Bordeaux which had been served much too cold; she should have opened it, permitted it to breathe before dinner. Next time—! *"Pierre!"*

Pierre let Nancy go, rather hastily taking her hand and touching his lips to it. "Tomorrow, *chérie*," he whispered. "We will find the apartment. Now, I must see what Claire wishes. In a moment she will call again, and I—"

It did not matter what he might have been going to say, nor that Nancy gave him no time to finish. She did not, however, intend to shove him so hard that he would lose his balance and fall back into the flower bed, cracking some bone against the wall. And maybe it was his bad leg, maybe she had really hurt him—but she did not look back. She did not look back until she was in the cab that had fortunately come by, and then she saw that Pierre was on his feet holding his arm as though it had been hurt. And that he was staring after her with the injured look of a man who has, perhaps for the first time in his life, been unfairly and certainly unpredictably attacked by a woman.

As for Nancy, she had no idea why she couldn't stop crying all the way back through the beautiful, brightly lighted, nighttime Paris streets.

The following day, an unexpected event found Mme Lévy at the pension table in a softer, less caustic mood: her son had sent money for a visit home to Philadelphia, her first in thirty years. Contemplating this, the old woman's eyes got a far-off look and sentimentally, as though she might never again return to this land of her dead French husband, she said, almost to herself: "Strange. It will be strange to hear one's native speech surrounding one again, even in one's most intimate moments. . . . I will have to adjust to that." Then her old eyes looked inward and she shook her head as though from incredulity. "For so long I have believed that it is only in the French tongue that words come truly from the heart."

"Is it?" Nancy asked, without much thought; but suddenly it came to her that which she had forgotten: that Pierre's loving letters had been in French and not in English; that he had not then written to practice his English *vocabulaire,* and that thus he could not have shown those letters to his Claire or she would have known this to be true. Claire was the one who had lied, and Pierre had told the truth! A different truth to each of them, as perhaps to every other woman in his life—but he had not lied.

Impulsively she turned to Mme Lévy. "You tried to tell me the truth about a Frenchman, Mme Lévy," she began; but she did not go on. The old woman looked as though she simply could not remember what Nancy might be talking about, and shrugged as though it were a pointless subject after all.

Course in the Language and Civilization of France

The first Monday morning Jane Dobie had left the Pension du Coeur for the École Française early enough, she'd thought, to be in good time for her class. But when she found the lobby and stairs already packed with students whose physical bodies crowded and multiplied with terrifying rapidity, she had nearly panicked before she reached her classroom on the top fifth floor. Like a log in turbulent rapids she'd been thrust back down the stairs again and again, so by the time the glass doors of Mme Caillaux's class at the top of the École Française finally closed behind her, she knew she could not go through such an ordeal another day.

The next morning she'd arrived early, hoping in this way to avoid the rush; but then she'd been trapped by a no less passionate surge of students stampeding upward. Nothing in all Jane's twenty-six years of easy American growth had given her strength to compete with those hard, determined European legs, nor had any will for learning she'd known equalled the passion of their quest.

Luckily, on the third day, she found a way to escape the mob simply by being late. Mme Caillaux, the volatile little French teacher, had glared briefly when Jane entered the classroom, but then, as though her tolerances extended even to a tardy American, had nodded and shrugged in forgiveness; no one else was concerned at all. This then, was the method Jane pursued on all the mornings after, happily, since the class of Mme Caillaux was exactly what she'd hoped to find for the few weeks she had in Paris.

The tiny Frenchwoman was not only a remarkably good teacher but also a colorful human being, with gamin charm and great intensity of purpose. Her likes and dislikes were equally impassioned, equally unrestrained, and her sunny blue eyes and squat, pleasure-loving figure aroused affection and loyalty in them which, after the first day's energetic session, never wavered. Yet it was, above all, the understanding she gave them of the French tongue which won their undivided allegiance; fighting for perfection every step of the way, she grimaced and pointed and scolded and mocked until the language beat and pulsed in their blood with the rhythm of their own hearts.

As for herself, she told them in the course of continuous and never quite irrevelant chatter, she worried about *rien!* As a Frenchwoman who had survived the German Occupation, who paid her own Party dues since twenty years, who had obtained her own divorce, and whose child was being wisely tutored by the good Catholic nuns of Notre-Dame-des-Champs, what need had she to ask *le bon Dieu* for more than He had given?—Except that He agitate this lazy class to spend more time on their *grammaire!*

"*D'accord?*" she would demand, holding out her child-like, nail-bitten hands like a militant saint, and they shouted back, "*D'accord!*" in unison, all bobbing happily their multilingual heads.

Now on this particular June day she sat before them with her short arms folded over her small protuberant belly, the black lead pencil reposing quietly, for once, in the roots of her rust-colored hair—like a molting hen perched upon her nest, thought Jane Dobie with affectionate regard—and observed the class beaming back at her from their benches. Mme Ruggiero and M. Kalinen in the second row leaned slightly forward, Mme Sienkiewicz and Mlle Engleman in the third row also, for these four were always well-prepared but inclined to interrupt each other. Senorita del Julio, third row left, was giggling with Lars Christensen who shared her *banc* (it was a mystery how she ever learned anything, always flirting as she was with the Danish boy), but they too looked devotedly at Mme Caillaux.

In the front row sat the stolid German girl, Anna, who tried so earnestly and learned so slowly, but accepted corrections with the sweet gravity of a child; and finally there was M. Zoltan, the stoop-shouldered, sad-faced Hungarian Freedom Fighter whose lessons were splendidly prepared but who stuttered when he recited—perhaps because he so seldom took his gaze from Miss Bourne-Jones, who noticed him not at all.

Mme Caillaux's eyes often turned toward the English girl's cameo-perfect face, her narrow bones encased in fine lavender tweed, the relaxed and slender hands marking her so unmistakably for the privileged aristocrat that she was. Such a creature would no doubt perish in the world Mme Caillaux envisaged for the future, a world dominated by Workers and the Communist Party, but in the meantime she seemed to take some pleasure in that pale perfection; and even Jane could imagine such delicate features and nubile grace better suited to the Eighteenth Century than to the Twentieth with its mass-production, mechanized ways, and increased tempo of life. . . . When, a moment after, the Frenchwoman's eyes turned as by some natural progression of thought from Miss Bourne-Jones to Jane, then passed on, it seemed that she conceded the American was more acceptable than some who represented the hated capitalistic States.

But in her classroom, Mme Caillaux permitted no prejudices to exist: not to others, not to herself. Here no student would be blamed for the sins of her or his own national leaders, here each was an individual equal to any other, and it was with no inconsistency at all that she, a loyal Communist, could nod with real affection for M. Zoltan, the Hungarian Freedom Fighter, to read next from the text.

He, poor fellow, had first to tear his eyes from the beautiful Miss Bourne-Jones before, in a nervously accented voice, he could begin. " 'Allons plus loin,' dit M. Vincent," he read, and everyone broke into laughter, for he had turned to the wrong page in the book.

"You go too far!" cried Mme Caillaux in scolding good humor, and M. Zoltan, blushing miserably, hastily found the correct place and read on with perspiration breaking out on his high, back-slanting forehead. But the June heat was now pouring in through the windows on this first really hot day of the year, and the lovely skin of Senorita del Jolio too was glistening like ripe rosy fruit, the white collar of M. Kalinen wilted visibly. Only Miss Bourne-Jones, it seemed, remained cool and undisturbed by the uncomfortably rising temperature.

It was M. Kalinen's turn next and he bounded to his feet to read, and to spar vigorously over his pronunciation with Mme Caillaux.

"Mais, regardez!" she scolded, thrusting her black pencil through her disordered hair until it seemed the scalp must be streaked with lead. "The lips spread on the segond vowel, not the première!" And time after time she made him try this, time after time she demonstrated by pursing her lips in the ridiculous caricature of a kiss, while the blond Danish boy, Lars, bounced in his seat, demanding to show that he knew how it was done.

"All right, you!" ordered Madame in great good humor, and the Dane, whose wide lips and broad forehead could not diminish the keen intelligence of his clear blue eyes nor the virile attractiveness of his apple-red cheeks, demonstrated before the class until even the pale, aristocratic Miss Bourne-Jones sat back limp with laughter. Mme Caillaux had to lean against her desk, lifting the coarse brown hem of her skirt (the same brown skirt day after day) to wipe laughter tears from her eyes and from her glasses before the clownish Dane started them off again. It is possible that the École Française had never before seen a more ridiculous use of classroom time, nor a mood which changed so suddenly, became something else so quickly.

At twenty before twelve, with an hour and ten minutes of the period to go, the door was opened by an extremely agitated director who asked Madame, rapidly, if he could bring someone or something into her classroom.

Jane Dobie understood this much, and that Madame refused at first, thrusting out her lower red lip and scowling, arching back her body and supporting herself by hands placed behind her on the desk. Her class was *parfait* as it was, she said antagonistically, and this which M. le Directeur requested would interfere with their progress, which she could not permit.

The nervous official kept explaining, however, in French so rapid that everyone but Mme Caillaux was lost.

"*Si vous voulez,*" she said at last, sulkily, and gave a reluctant shrug. "Let them come, *mais—je ne l'aime pas!*"

She then walked behind her desk and slouched in her

chair like a child that has been unfairly chastized, and the class, aroused, waited for the new students who, presumably, would appear. There was some movement outside the glass as vaguely defined figures, like insects attracted by a light, seemed pressing against the door, but for a long moment no one came in.

At last Madame aroused herself and in a loud aside to the class said sarcastically: "They are afraid we will eat them!" Then she ran the pencil lead through her top hair and called so she could be heard outside the closed door and perhaps down the stairs and on the floor below as well: "What is it that holds you there, cowards? *Entrez donc!*"

The door was thrust open by a sharp-featured, thin-bodied man wearing a formal dark suit and white collar reminiscent of another generation, his black hair sleekly parted to one side, his tight nostrils suggesting an alert rodent. Briefly his eyes rested on the class before he stood aside for the restless creatures they saw massed behind him.

The class watched with varying reactions as eight or ten sullen men and women swarmed into the room and filled it with heavy breathing as of young animals brought in from the fields; and young these creatures were, whether they had thinning hair, paunches beneath their sweaters and dresses, or the narrow, pinched lips of under-privileged adolescents. Even the women with dry skin covered by heavy makeup, or no makeup at all, were no older than twenty or thirty, although some looked forty. And no one, neither the hostile intruders nor the established class of Mme Caillaux attempted any smiles or friendly looks.

M. Zoltan made the first move. He stood abruptly beside his bench and hesitated only an instant, staring down at Miss Bourne-Jones as though pleading with her to follow. There was even a flicker of response in the English girl's cool eyes, but everything happened too fast, and the next instant M. Zoltan turned to hurry alone across the room with his head down, almost tripping over the foot of a large young man, who then noisily took the seat beside Miss Bourne-Jones.

Mme Caillaux, after allowing a full five minutes for the disturbance to die down and the dark-haired, cold-faced leader of the invaders to take a seat to one side, moved forward into command. *"Attention!* You will now, please, open the books!" She stood before them like a top sergeant, her hands planted on her broad, solid hips, leaving no doubt of her authority. But then she smiled, almost naturally; after all, she identified herself with the *ouvriers* and *jeunesse* of any nation and the intellectual challenge and needs of these young Communists from the East must be met and welcomed. Other groups had come throughout the winter, wisely brought from their homelands for Party work well-done—it was not their fault that such French as had been taught them before they came was so *mal entendu.*

Although most of the group were holding the new blue books given them in the office below, they did not seem to understand what Mme Caillaux had said. Only half did as they were told while the others maintained an antagonistic silence and impassivity that brought a strange uneasiness into this room; until suddenly a new voice spoke loudly: *"Quels beaux yeux!"*

Immediately all eyes turned toward the swarthy young man beside Miss Bourne-Jones, who was now staring at her in frank delight. His shoulders in the patterned sweater were solid as a farm boy's, his neck was muscular as a wrestler's, and his hair was thick-black and curly, with a small bald spot on the crown; and his heavy arm was curving in confident familiarity across the slender back of the English girl who sat as one frozen, incapable of drawing herself away. Then, almost like normal youth, some of his companions laughed aloud.

Mme Caillaux seemed about to make a pleasantry—after all, when French is spoken impulsively, that is good, is it not?—until she observed the gathering tension reflected in the faces of Miss Bourne-Jones's classmates. Nervously then she looked down at her book, without comment. "You must take the dictation now," she ordered, and began to read from the text in a firm voice, pausing occasionally to frown over the tops of her glasses at the recurring shuffling of feet, as though she might yet report these students to a higher authority. "Be quiet, please," she said, frequently, interrupting herself.

The swarthy young man kept staring at Miss Bourne-Jones as at some precious jewel unexpectedly placed within his reach. So must the first peasant to enter the Czar's palace have stared on seeing unimagined treasure, so he was now staring with unmistakable delight. Not until the girl drew away, as though her acquiescence had been merely good manners and not acceptance, did the settled members of the class sit back in relief; if one of them were menaced, it seemed they all must be. (It was not that M. Zoltan did not count, but he'd had no alternative than to leave.)

Observing the faint moisture incongruously appearing under the smooth back hair on Miss Bourne-Jones's white, seemingly poreless neck, Jane saw that the moment had, after all, cost the girl some strain. It would have been better if she'd left with M. Zoltan earlier—although this rough stranger could surely not disturb her long, in spite of his uninhibited male admiration and farcical broad humor. She was protected enough in Mme Caillaux's classroom, even though the time moved now so slow; but why didn't the little teacher suggest that the unpleasant fellow change his seat?

"*Attention!*" Mme Caillaux cried again, this time with new and formidable vigor, and the regular class turned back to its lessons, almost reassured. She was still *maîtresse*; but neither her authority nor their confidence could last for long. From the rear they heard another exclamation, louder than any of the preceding, which this time brought the Frenchwoman angrily marching down the aisle to face a grim young man whose large hooked nose was like a weapon between angry, mocking eyes.

"Why you do that?" she cried. "How is it you behave this way? In France, you have no manners, *alors?* This reward they give, you come to Paris!—Why you not be good?"

The big-nosed man stared contemptuously and then tossed his new blue book across the room so that the swarthy young man beside Miss Bourne-Jones had to duck it, or pretend that he did, with a rich yell of pleasure.

"Funny, no?" he cried in English, his hand squeezing delightedly on the girl's shoulder, and astonishingly a small, assenting smile appeared on her startled face.

Poor Mme Caillaux, who had met nothing like this before, retreated behind her desk muttering angrily to herself and began turning the pages back to the beginning of the text. One could see her blue eyes dart in desperation through the heavy glasses and her hand with the black lead pencil trembling; but what could they do to help her?

"We will review," she said, her voice lower than usual, but for an instant she looked reproachfully at the dark-suited leader sitting with such calm detachment in his seat. "Conjugate *être,*" she pleaded, to anyone, passing the palm of her hand down over the brown wool skirt. Since no one else responded, Jane Dobie raised her hand.

At first Mme Caillaux looked as though she would reject the American, but as there were no other hands she shrugged, her eyes unexpectedly warming. "You, Mrs. Dobie. Yes, you, please!"

Where there had been noise before there was now silence, the air heavy with hostility as everyone stared at the American they had not been worldly or traveled enough to recognize before. Only the leader's face did not change, since he, of course, had understood all along that she was the enemy.

"*Je suis, tu es, il est*," began Jane, speaking neither far back in her throat as the English, nor trillingly, as Senorita del Jolio would have done: she spoke as an American who has been well-trained, but still could never be taken for French. In the quiet, it seemed everyone listened—everyone but Mme Caillaux, who stared into space and forgot to tell Jane to stop and let someone else take over.

So Jane went to the *passé simple* and *passé composé*, the *conditionnel* and then the *subjonctif*, with her voice becoming thin and breathless as the silence continued without mercy in the increasingly heated room. Then another textbook fell, or was thrown, crashing onto the floor.

As if by accident the next one dropped too, then another, while the dark-haired leader sat as though devoid of any interest in their behavior, as though he were perhaps, a member of the original class of Mme Caillaux. Yet when the distraught teacher pounded on her desk at last, crying, "You will take up your books!" and cast on him a desperate look of appeal, he slowly turned those cold, fanatical eyes upon his charges, and as though he threatened them, they picked up the books, either those they had thrown or others which they handed back to the owners, so that by the time Jane sat down, shaken more than she would have imagined from her ordeal, a certain order seemed to have been restored.

Yet now they all saw that Mme Caillaux was close to hysteria. Talking to herself and on the verge of tears, she held her large common wristwatch before her eyes as though with difficulty making out the hands; but the end was not yet in sight, and Jane wondered if she could go on.

She could, of course. They all saw the sudden disciplined tightening of facial muscles as, jabbing the black pencil even more wildly through her hair, the Frenchwoman walked over to a girl seated in front of the class who had, so far, taken no part in the disturbances. This girl too was one of the Communists, yet she seemed not quite one of them, either: something about the almost stylish cut of her sweater and skirt, the bleached hair worn smooth across her forehead and the small-stoned child's ring on her third finger gave her a look of greater privilege, greater sophistication than the rest. She was even, in a sulky way, conventionally pretty, and her eyes had rested observingly on the English girl from time to time as one woman will who observes the style of another. Surely, thought Jane, she can and will help Mme Caillaux through the time that is left.

" '*Avez-vous une soeur?*' " read Mme Caillaux hopefully, and pointed at the girl and the unopened book in her lap. But as the girl stared back without answering, she somehow seemed the most insolent one of all. To the small desperate Frenchwoman, it was almost more than she could stand. "*Voila!*" she ordered. "You have the book! You have study the *française*, now you answer me! Say '*oui*' or '*non!*' " And she jabbed wildly at her hair with the pencil; but it was no use.

"*Non!*" said the girl, contemptuously. "*Non,*" she repeated defiantly, then turned her cold young face to the window, while in the room behind there was stirring as though the animals in the cage were becoming restless enough to break their bonds.

It was when the black pencil finally ceased darting through the disordered coiffure that one saw Madame's defeat. Her bright child's air of being equal to anyone in laughter, in fighting, or in love, was no longer on her face or in her manner; and (though surely the rich must be condemned, the poor be loved, the downtrodden raised and the ignorant be given light) when the dregs rise back into the wine, where could a poor Frenchwoman turn for renewal of the faith?

For the rest of the period, Mme Caillaux quietly read aloud, pretending not to care if anyone understood or responded or even listened, ignoring interruptions while the swarthy man in the ugly sweater kept murmuring in a persistent, wooing way to Miss Bourne-Jones who amazingly, at that moment, seemed the only one still undisturbed. She shared her book with him, her slender shoulders in the lavender tweed subtly inclined toward the tree-trunk solidity of the man, while the voice of Mme Caillaux, somehow diminished, droned on as though forever.

All but Mme Caillaux heard the closing bell, but she went right on reading as they began rising noisily from their seats. Only minutes later did she look up and cry: "The bell?—I did not hear the bell!" Her glasses slipped to the end of her short brave nose and she could not stop protesting. "Always I hear the bell! You are *sure?*" She was still shaking her head as though some deep illusions of herself had been destroyed when Jane reached the door, where the dark-eyed leader of the tribe stood waiting.

Very softly, he spoke to her. "*Au revoir,*" he said. Then with a small, almost gallant bow: "*À bientôt,* Mrs. Dobie."

"*Au revoir,*" she returned hastily and moved on, thinking, Why did I speak to him, after the way he let those creatures behave with Mme Caillaux? *À bientôt*—until we meet again?—What did he mean by that? He heard my name from Mme Caillaux; but why did he speak to *me?*

"That I did not hear the bell!" she heard the French-

woman still fretting behind her as she stepped out on the
landing above the stairs, which were not yet crowded, but
the doors were being opened rapidly, and in no time at all
she was pushed right to the railing by the first surge of students bolting from their classrooms. Running with the tide
as more men and women poured from the fourth and then
the third floor into the mainstream, Jane felt herself tossed
like a small bark where many tributaries ran together, flooding banks which so far had held. To her right she saw Lars
Christensen and the Spanish girl jostled too, but holding
hands as unconcerned as ever. . . . It could happen on a day
like this, she thought suddenly as she was swept along by
the rushing bodies with the deafening roar of voices in her
ears. We could all be going along in the mainstream when
the break comes and the railings give way, plunging us
down to destruction.

In panic, she drew back into the stifling mob, and someone whose foot she stepped on, swore; momentarily she was
delayed, long enough for others to crowd ahead of her. So
it was a moment later that she saw, some steps below, the
fair head of Miss Bourne-Jones with the black-haired young
man from the classroom close beside her. His sweatered arm
was around the girl, and in one startled moment it seemed
to Jane that the lavender tweed on her shoulder had been
torn. But the next wave brought her a step nearer, and she
saw that the only violation of Miss Bourne-Jones's elegance
was the broad hand of the invader on the lavender tweed,
pushing her his way. The curious thing, though, was that
on the English girl's perfect lips, there was, unmistakably,
a new and secret smile of consent.

A sudden clearing, and there on the landing below she
saw the face of M. Zoltan, turned upward with a look as
yearning as when he had read in class: " 'Allons plus loin,'
dit M. Vincent."

"*Plus loin?*" No, thought Jane suddenly, the Hungarian didn't go too far, it's just that the rest of us didn't go far enough; and it seemed this was something of vital importance that she must communicate to the English girl— but it was too late. Miss Bourne-Jones and her companion were far ahead now, and M. Zoltan had vanished in the flood of the faceless crowd.

The Thief on the
Champs Élysées

Standing before the kiosk waiting for a copy of *l'Express*, I suddenly felt my big leather handbag weightless as an empty pillowcase, and I did not have to look inside to know I had been robbed by the girl in the Prisunic.

My first impulse was to cry out to the *agent de police* standing like a giant gull flapping his cape wings at the turbulent six o'clock traffic from his island on the Champs Élysées. But by the time I had taken a step forward he had blown his whistle at a stalled motorist and had begun to shout such invective that, naturally, I reconsidered. A man too deep in any role does not care to be interrupted; it was doubtful, anyway, if he would consider a petty crime in a French five-and-dime store of any great importance.

There was a second, younger *agent* watching like an understudy from a window of a stationary police car, but seeing his concentration, I knew that to neither of them could I give way to hysteria. So I turned back to the kiosk, handed over the one franc for my newspapers (leaving only four new francs in my change purse), then spent another twenty-five centimes for *Le Figaro*. But my poise vanished at the moment this last coin left my hand and I raced back to the corner entrance of the Prisunic.

The doorway now was blocked by two dogs and a crowd of shoppers hilariously observing the somewhat distracted attempts of a large proletarian mongrel and a small, aristocratic white poodle to mate. It was only when the mongrel was dragged away by the nervous lad who was his master that the mistress of the elegant poodle managed to restrain her little bitch; but still the public remained to laugh and discuss *l'affaire* with the poodle's mistress, a cunningly designed bitch herself, in white wool and pink makeup.

"Naughty, naughty," she cried, and wagged her own white derriere in unison with her pets' as though she herself had felt the challenge of the attack.

"Excuse, please. *Excusez-moi!*" I pleaded, pushing against the crowd. Resentfully they let me through, their faces plainly saying, Here is another American tourist possessed of not a shred of feeling for the most amusing facts of life.

As it was only by pushing and struggling that I got through to the counter where, a moment ago, I had been trying on a cheap, ridiculous hat, I refused to be intimidated by the crowd. Yet the *vendeuse*, once I had attracted her attention, stared as though she had never seen me before, and for a moment this took all courage from me.

"Didn't you see the German girl?" I cried, breaking in on another customer. "The one beside me a moment ago? When I tried on these hats? Did you see her leave? Do you know which way she went?" I speak an American French, it is true, but surely she understood.

Handing a straw cloche to the customer, she retorted: "*Je ne comprends pas!*" I am ordinarily a coward before antagonism and I trembled, but did not retreat.

*   *   *

"I no understan'," the German girl had said to me in English—but that was before she had asked, "You do not find a hat you like?" with so little accent that I thought she was a fellow American presuming on our nationality; also I had not cared for the way she was crowding up against me. Then I turned and saw the foreign look. Although her soiled blond hair was cut in the same style as mine, it was clinging moistly to a broad square forehead; and, while the skin was young, it was marred by imperfections, as though she did not eat regularly or well. Yet there was also a familiarity about the face which puzzled me. Had I perhaps seen her at the École Française (she had seemed to know me by sight), or did she resemble some person I had known in the past?

I recalled that a traveling American must be friendly with all strangers, so I managed a distant but polite smile, at the same time drawing away from the touch of the girl's heavy coat against my bare arm (after all, it was a warm day in early September).

"The head sizes are too small for me," I replied, an admission which sometimes sounds boastful but always makes me think a cow's head is larger than a monkey's.

The girl disappeared, but, to my surprise, she reappeared at my right side. And she looked at me coldly then as though she'd not been the one to speak first and could not now imagine why I spoke to her at all!

"I no understan'," she said, with such a marked, guttural accent I wondered if I had been mistaken, if it had been someone else who had spoken before. Then the next instant like a whitecapped wave dissolved by the swell of the sea, the girl vanished into the crowd, having by then extracted my passport folder from the handbag over my left arm.

*   *   *

"I've been robbed," I tried to say calmly to the saleswoman. I leaned across the counter to bring my words
closer and clearer to her, for I could not allow her to ignore
me. "The girl who stood here a moment ago—You saw her!
You spoke to her and to me."

The *vendeuse* shrugged and coolly turned to rearrange her
hats on the shelves as though the subject were closed—as
though the girl I had spoken of, so far as she remembered
this day or any other, had never existed.

Nervous tears rose in my eyes and turning quickly I
knocked my frail paper bag, filled with objects I'd bought,
against the counter, where it broke. (So many things which
should be strong in France are frail, like paper bags, and
things thought to be weak are granite, like this woman.)
My small gifts for friends scattered like hailstones, the cans
of goose liver and pork pâté, the glass beads, pink soap,
scarves, and perfume bottles with flower-trimmed necks,
rolled, cluttered, fluttered or crashed into the aisle, and one
passing Frenchwoman was hit on the foot by a perfume vial
in the shape of a pig. I stooped to retrieve the nearest arti-
cles, thrusting these into my empty handbag (where my
passport folder had been the hour before), then retreated
into the crowd to lean against a counter where the red, blue,
green and yellow hats whirled into a spectrum of undistin-
guishable colors before my eyes.

I had not gone back to my French class on the Left Bank
that afternoon after the fitting of my Chantilly lace dress
at Mlle Boucicault's on the Boulevard Haussmann because I
felt too elevated by my glorified appearance in the dark
mirror to settle down to another daily battle of French
verbs in company with other accents as rusty as my own.
There, in the dim room where the little seamstress strained
her eyes, I had seen myself as I could be: my square brow
almost distinguished looking, my dark blond hair Rapun-

zelian, and my full face luminous as a photograph of the Princess d'X in the last issue of *Réalités;* so I rebelled. However, like many rebels, I had no cause, so the best thing I could think of was to go to a movie on the Champs Élysées.

Then, since the black lace gown was costing me twenty dollars more than I'd put aside for it, I passed up a film I wanted to see for a grade B picture made for French consumption only (there being a difference of four new francs between the two), and the dialogue in this was incomprehensible, the plot confused and the setting regional. I had walked out before the end with still an hour of freedom before I was expected back at the pension for the evening meal, when I noticed the Prisunic doors were open and I decided this was an unexpected opportunity to purchase small gifts to take back home.

My loose change was quickly gone, and it was necessary to take out the passport folder where I kept large bills— with my American Express checks, my Pan American plane ticket, vaccination certificate and other personal papers. Unfortunately, in order to remove one ten-franc note, I had to expose all, including the green end of my American passport; and while this had never bothered me before that moment I felt a curious sense of impending danger.

I could not reasonably explain this, nor can I now, yet it was as though some magnetic force were drawing that folder from my hands; and the sensation was so physical and so intense that after I had replaced the folder my arm actually ached. I recall rubbing my shoulder in alarm as though the strain had drawn heavily on the muscles of my heart, and then, as now, it seemed that I might faint. . . .

Now again, a weakness came over me, and I fell into that pit of clairvoyance where the sense of danger is as staggering as a drop from a precipice in a dream. So I understood quite clearly that by the time I'd put my folder out of sight it had already, in effect, been stolen by a thief in the Prisunic.

The weakness passed and anger returned as I opened my eyes on the increasing disorder of the milling French crowd with the dinner hour beginning to stir their bellies and their tempers. My impulse was now to get away, let it go, make out the best I could; but I thought if only someone would help me, I might still be able to find the German girl and force her to return my passport folder. After all, I was in a bad way without it.

"Where does one find the manager?" I asked another saleswoman, politely, but since she was concluding a sale and I had made her lose count of the change, she too stared in resentment. Then someone directed me to a long white basement passageway in the rear, and, turning my back upon the crowd, I entered upon a stretch of white walls and utter, unexpected silence in a passageway that must have tunneled far back under a city block.

Here was no visible exit other than the way I had come (the three doors I passed, running down the corridor, seemed closed and locked forever), but at the far end where I made a turn to the left I found a heavy door bolted like a vault. There was a smell of dryness here as from a well-stoked furnace and it seemed to me this might have been a gas chamber in the days of the Nazi Occupation; certainly I had been misdirected, so I turned and ran quickly back, down the white hall until, seeing one of the three doors open, I paused and looked inside to meet the eyes of a man standing over a white porcelain urinal. For one awful instant we both stared, unable to break the lock of mutual horror, then I fled through the door and out into the street.

The *agent* in the police car now was facing the other way, dreaming over orange umbrellas spread open like exotic fruits above the green tables of a café, but as I ran toward him his eyes turned and examined me with mild interest.

"A thief! *Une voleuse!*" I cried, before I again lost my nerve. "*Monsieur, s'il vous plâit*—I have been robbed in the Prisunic!"

He jumped out of his car at once, spoke rapidly to the officer on the safety island, and then entered the store with me. There he asked questions to right and to left so imperiously that in spite of the same blank stares as before, I was charmed and encouraged by his authority. And the hat saleswoman, this time, was not so indifferent, even though she still denied having seen anyone beside me at the counter in the past hour. There had been only one "*etrangère,*" she insisted, since noon: this one (who was I).

Like searching for a pebble on a rocky shore when the tide has come and gone, we wandered from counter to counter until the female manager appeared from the depths to pronounce any theft here *impossible.* If Mam'selle would only produce the proof, she said, or perhaps if I looked again in my bag, I would find the object which I thought I had lost.

"I did not lose anything," I said, firmly. "My passport folder with my identification, my money, everything I own, was stolen in this store. I only wish help in finding the German girl who stood beside me." I pointed out the saleswoman. "It seems very strange that *she* will not admit this."

The manager continued to shake her head as other customers gathered around, and some were friendly to me, a stranger in trouble, and some were not, seeing I was American. But the young policeman stood steady and unflinching as a rock, coming back again and again with his sharp, hard questions; then we were again on the street, the store closing for the night, and nothing had been accomplished.

I waited beside my defender as he consulted a new, small

book. "*Le Commissariat*. Ah," he murmured, his finger moving down the pages, then all at once I understood he must be very new in the service, or he would not be so eager to help, and so uninformed. His uniform too was fresh, new, unwrinkled, his shoes and belt highly polished (doubtless even his gun was still untried!); then, as I watched, his hard round chin puckered, his Norman blue eyes brightened, and even his tan mustache lifted with a charming smile.

Moistening his red lips, he showed me what he had been looking for in the book. "We go there!" he said, and we set off together on the rue Balzac where he made a sharp left into the rue Lord Byron, and then a sharp right, like an excited school boy in search of a darting squirrel. Tonight he would no doubt return to his parents (I decided he was too young and thoughtless for wife and child) who would listen to his prattle about an American woman who had carried in her handbag as much money as a Frenchman spends in a year for his wine; and then I caught the eye of a passer-by and understood that I myself could seem to be a criminal, dragged along by the police! Once again I had the impulse to bolt, but by then it was too late. Unexpectedly my companion asked, with some concern, "*Ça va bien?*" And my face must surely have been a mess, red and soiled, with my hair hanging limp as the German thief's across her forehead.

"*Ça va*," I returned crossly, but then he moved to the outer edge of the walk and motioned me on ahead, apparently deciding at last that it was safe to be more agreeable. After that we walked along as equals, talking of this thing that had happened to me, he even understanding my French, and I—since he spoke with peasant slowness—understanding his. The accidental meeting of our eyes was so agreeable that by the time we reached the Commissariat on the Faubourg-du-Roule in the 8th Arrondissement we were remarkably at ease with one another, so that my protector introduced me to the elder of the two officers as tenderly as though we had been in love.

A small Algerian standing before the court tapped lightly and respectfully on the counter. "*Je vous prie, Monsieur le Commissaire.* We stand here first. Hear me, please," he requested, and his sullen woman twisted a finger through a black curl, narrowing her eyes at me. But the officials were more interested in my case and spoke in such a way that the poor couple moved back to a bench against the wall with the resignation of those who must always wait on official favor.

Now, with gallantry, my officer began our story, and I was pleased that he told it so well, encouraged by his superiors who listened like elders sponsoring a young man and are delighted at his making good. The second official, however, had to leave for his dinner and rose, shaking hands with his colleague, nodding approvingly and encouragingly at the gendarme, and at the door his eyes lingered a moment upon my legs and this also seemed friendly and human. Then we got down to the business of the theft.

The Commissaire stated his passionate regret that I, an American guest of Paris, had been treated so badly. That I, a lovely lady, must understand that Paris was really not a lawless city—not like New York, which our own Mayor, interviewed last week by *France-Soir,* had admitted to be shockingly full of unsolved crimes.

At this moment a small and humble detective came in on my case, with a dog nervy and tail-wagging as any stray along a country road, and although one could hardly take either of them seriously, the dog's tongue dripped with anticipation, his eyes glistened, and he pulled on the leash as though eager to get on with the chase. I could not understand why they returned back through the door through which they had come—which could not possibly lead to the Prisunic—since I had been requested to give the dog a friendly sniff of my hand which held the bag.

I did not wish, however, to criticize Monsieur le Commissaire, who was certainly doing his best. Even now he was writing out a report for the American Embassy, a favor I had not thought of asking.

"They will be *très, très agité*," he said. "A passport is taken seriously by your Government, Madame. And by ours," he added hastily.

Then he asked if I had enough francs for my dinner, putting his hand in his pocket, and I was touched by this, but explained that I was perhaps still expected at my pension, late as it was. At that he himself telephoned Mlle du Coeur, conversing with her in the polished manner she prefers, and when he bowed me away at last it seemed as though we had met in social surroundings and only incidentally were in these drab police headquarters which, now that I thought about it, had the smell of frightful but detected crimes.

At the last moment my eyes met those of my policeman (whose name I never knew!), seeing his expression so regretful, his red lips so moist and his eyes so soft and brooding that it seemed something profoundly emotional had been shared between us in this most exceptional hour of our intimacy. He even took a step toward me, impulsively as a lover wishing to keep me from leaving—but it was too fragile a thing between us, and the older man, sympathetically but firmly, reached out and put a restraining hand upon his arm.

As I passed the Algerian couple stirring hopefully on their bench, I felt quite misty-eyed, and it was not until I found myself again on the darkening street, the lamps now

lighted, that I remembered the thief herself had not, after
my first description, been referred to by anyone again.

Back at the pension I was greeted with excitement, and
there was a small supper which Mlle du Coeur had placed in
my room, ham and cheese and an orange from Spain, with
my own bottle of cold white wine, a clean napkin wrapped
about its neck. So when I went to bed at last I felt com-
forted as a child after a storm of tears. It was not until
much later, in my dreams, I found the German girl beside
me once more, somehow increasingly familiar, the same
height as myself, although she had seemed less tall the hours
before. And my sense of well-being vanished, so that I
wept, awakening with a sense of loss more personal and disturbing than any I had ever known.

Lightheartedness briefly returned next day when the Pan
American Airlines gave me another ticket, and a Frenchman
at the American Express issued new travelers checks to me
equal in value to those stolen with my passport.

"We may ask you later to identify any forgeries," he
said, and I begged to be allowed to do this, to do anything
to show my gratitude. I also suggested that the checks be
particularly watched for in Germany, since the thief had
spoken with a German accent.

"Would you give me a brief description?" he asked, although I thought I had done this.

"She was about my height," I said, "and also my coloring.
It is even possible that if we dressed alike she might somehow resemble me." This I said on the impulse of the moment, for it had not occurred to me before. I could not
understand why the young man seemed startled at what I
said.

Then at the American Consulate I discovered the precari-

ous balance of my situation, for I failed to be received with
any friendliness at all.

"A lost passport," said the narrow-chinned, pale-lipped
woman official, "places the guilt squarely upon the loser,
Mrs. Greenhill."

"But I did not lose it! Here is the report of the Commissioner of Police," I said, thrusting the document across her
desk. "This is the proof if there is any doubt in your mind."

But the woman only looked at me with further dislike
and touched the tip of a pointed tongue to her upper lip,
shaking her head. "This only says that you reported your
passport stolen: I fail to see any *proof*. I can only repeat, an
American passport is not a thing to be treated lightly."

"I went to the police—and they believed me!" But I saw
then I was being accused of something.

"Those Frenchmen can be fooled," she said, briefly. "We
cannot."

"I have my reservation to go home on Friday," I said,
fighting for control. "I must have a passport—I cannot possibly stay in Paris any longer!"

"We are not a Welfare Agency," said the woman, coldly.

"Everyone has been helpful," I protested. "Even the
Commissioner of Police offered to lend me francs for my
dinner." Yet when I saw the nasty look on her face I knew
I had been foolish to say this.

"I doubt that an officer of the French Government would
lend money to any woman—except at a price!" she said
dryly, and I saw we were fighting the most primitive battle
of all, the generosity of men toward one kind of woman
and not to another.

"If I don't have my passport by Friday, I will lose my
reservation and—perhaps more," I said quietly. I could not
tell her I was going home to a man I had almost divorced,
and that I could not now bear to wait another hour. She

would have no more sympathy for that kind of nonsense than for any other. "Please—surely there is something you can do."

So, finally, perhaps trapped by my false humility, the woman stared with resentful eyes and told me to return on Wednesday. "With photos, and accompanied by someone to identify you. In the meantime—try to find your passport."

On Wednesday I went back with three photos and an acquaintance from the pension who carried driver's license, insurance papers, personal mail and an American library card: but, alas, she had forgotten to bring her own passport, which was in her husband's coat pocket. The assistant consul became quite cheery when she discovered this and sent me away again empty-handed, saying to come back on Thursday.

But Thursday turned out to be a holiday, which I had not foreseen, nor, perhaps, had she. So the acquaintance and I, who had hurried through breakfast in order to appear at nine-thirty, were turned away again. There had been rain in the night, and when we saw it still looked threatening, the lady from the pension decided to go right back to her room. I found a small café a block from the Consulate and sat there over coffee, brooding. Who and what I was if I had been asked to prove my existence at that moment, I did not know, for it seemed one could not exist without papers and the official approval of the baleful, cold-natured assistant lady consular employee. But the thief, I thought suddenly, the German girl, how easy it must be now for her! All she has to say is: Here is *my* passport, *my* money, *my* checks, and she will be honored, while I, who can be identified only by my face, my bones and my speech, am unaccepted, accused of not telling the truth.

But the thought of that girl intrigued me. Perhaps she

has a lover, I thought, a Frenchman; and since Friday at six P.M. they must have spent many of those crisply decorative, new ten-franc notes. The girl also, surely, will have bought a new, lighter coat and had her blond hair washed. And if her lover *is* a Frenchman they will also have eaten good food and drunk fine wines, which even so soon as this may have improved the texture of her skin.

Yet I no longer had francs in my pocket, and the lace dress would have to be canceled, that pale, transfigured face rising from the mirror of Mlle Boucicault forgotten as though it had never been. . . .

Feeling intense self-pity, seeing again that mirror which now reflected no image of myself at all, I was relieved when an American Army man I'd met the week before came by and sat down beside me. Listening to my unhappy story he, being a man of action, at once took charge. Even though it was a holiday, he got up from the table and telephoned a friend in the Embassy and stormed about my treatment, saying if something was not done *"toute suite,"* he'd raise holy hell! If they gave me a runaround this time, I heard him say, "By God, we'll move in with the Army!"

Thus the next morning I was received quickly by the assistant lady consul, and although she found one last way of annoying me (my pictures were not acceptable and I must go to a photographer down the street who charged three times the ordinary fee), I stood before her at last, complete with all requirements. She looked at my witness's documents, she looked at the forms I had filled in, and she looked at my newest photo.

"This doesn't look like you," she complained, but now only as someone forced to accept irritating reality. And certainly the photo did not: with that harassed look on my face and my neglected blond hair, I resembled more the German thief than I did myself!

Yet I managed to keep my tongue, even when she gave me a passport good for only six days, although I was laughing hysterically when I went, for the last time, out the Consulate door.

Back in New York at last, I remained grateful to the French policeman and the Commissaire, to Mlle du Coeur, to Pan American, the American Express and to the Major of the American Army. I told the story several times about the unkindness of the American consul's assistant, and friends said I should write to my congressman or to the newspapers, which I never did. I was glad to be home, and happy, and managed to put the whole thing from my mind. Until one morning four months later, when a letter came from a Mr. Brown at the Express Company asking me to call and identify signatures on checks I had reported lost in Paris.

Feeling oddly relieved that here at last was proof that I had been robbed, I telephoned and said I would be delighted to come down, although I hadn't really thought the checks would ever be returned.

"Why not?" Mr. Brown asked. I did not know, I said, although I supposed it was because of the German girl.

"Were you in Germany then, Mrs. Greenhill? I understood you were only in France."

This seemed irrelevant, but I explained it was a German girl who had stolen them from my handbag in the Prisunic.

"I did not know that," he said. Somewhat hastily, I said I would be right down.

I was delayed by various duties so that it was three hours before I ascended the old-fashioned elevator and entered a room which seemed the sum total of all official rooms in the world. I'd been in quite a number since I'd started this search for my possessions, the police station in the Fau-

bourg-du-Roule, the Express office in Paris, the Consulate
—all cheerless, repelling blocks of granite challenge to un-
proven claims of humanity.

"I'm expected," I said to the girl at the switchboard, and
a young man stood half-way down that big room and motioned to me. His face was reassuringly young, although
blank and smooth, and expressionless eyes gave me a searching look of inspection before we sat down. Then he opened
a folder on his desk and placed it on my lap.

"There are the checks, Mrs. Greenhill," he said. "Please
examine them carefully. Tell me, if you can, which signatures are real and which are fraudulent."

"Zürich!" I exclaimed. "They speak German there—at
least I was not wrong about the girl's accent."

"All our checks are cleared through Zürich," he informed
me, as though I had said something stupid. "Now, the signatures—please."

There was my name at the top of each check as I had
signed it in my own bank and there was the counter-signa-
ture in the lower right hand corner, also in my handwriting
—small, impatient, too rapid for style, and too slanting, I
have been told, for emotional stability. And all of these
signatures, there was no doubt about it, must be mine.

"They look all right," I said, thinking this was some
trick to show me only my own signed checks; then I
counted them, and saw there were far too many here for
that.

"Please look again, Mrs. Greenhill. This is a very serious
matter."

I picked up the checks one by one, examining each letter,
becoming so absorbed that I did not at once notice a woman
who joined us. But when I looked up to say that it was still
absurdly difficult to swear I had not written them all, she
was looking over his shoulder with the same bright, ob-

servant, accusing smile I'd last seen on the face of the woman assistant consul in Paris. "Mrs. Saks," said Mr. Brown.

It was important they both understand, so I began to tell them all the circumstances of the theft. This thief on the Champs Élysées who had been so clever as to master my signature was a dull-looking creature as she'd stood beside me in the Prisunic, I said. So how could they explain this thing the German girl had done—mastering an imitation of my handwriting which had been shaped by my own three hundred years of American environment? Were there no national differences any more? I went distractedly on, about the girl and me at opposite poles, and how she had stood there trying on a hat and watching me—but the *vendeuse* had claimed she remembered only one of us.

"Mrs. Greenhill, will you please, once more, describe this girl."

"Yes, of course." But suddenly I faltered, my face grew hot and I found myself snapping the catch on my small city handbag. And although I needed a cigarette, I dared not reach for one, knowing that my hand would tremble. For the truth was now that I could not remember the face of the girl nor evoke her in my mind. Even as I tried to say the words I thought I had said before—blonde, my height, a wide, square forehead, round flushed face, brown eyes—it seemed I was describing not a stranger, but myself!

Then again it was as it had been in the Prisunic when I was fighting for possession against a will strong enough to draw my life's blood, challenging my own right to keep what was privately and exclusively my own. Now, again, it seemed I was protecting something perhaps less tangible but of even greater value: my own belief in myself. "The man at the Express office in Paris believed me, you know," I said,

wretchedly, seeing plainly enough what they all were thinking. *"He* did not once suggest I might have lost it—"

"Nor have we," said Mr. Brown, exchanging glances with
the woman. "Even though there have been no other thefts
reported in that district for a year."

"A year ago," said Mrs. Saks, "a French woman with a
red purse did a job in that store. Yet it is hard to see how a
German girl could have escaped without attracting more
attention."

There is no German girl, they seemed to say, where is
your proof? Here are the checks you reported lost and the
others the foolish Frenchman in our office gave you—but
the signatures, you see, are all the same.

Then unexpectedly Mr. Brown leaned forward and
touched one finger to the smaller pile of checks. "Those are
the forgeries, Mrs. Greenhill. You will observe the movement of the pen on the final letters, and how the 'r' is not
the same. So there is nothing more we need ask of you at
this moment—although since two are still missing we may
call on you again. Thank you for coming in."

The trial was ended, and they meant for me to go. But
this was not fair; I could see even then that they had not
taken my word for all this, and I wanted to prove it to
them, and to the young policeman and the Commissaire
who had looked so sad to have me leave—for they had not
believed me, either: I understood that at last. I was the only
one who had seen the German girl, who could not now be
properly described. Yet, she was still abroad in the world,
still uncommitted and still free—my deadliest enemy, who
had stolen my money, my passport, and my face.

Schenectady Yawns
Before Us

At noon on the twenty-sixth of August, Lester Clarke left the Sorbonne as usual for his lunch at the Pension du Coeur. After the hot uncomfortable summer the air seemed fresh, almost cool, and as he entered the gates of the Luxembourg Gardens the park appeared before him like a painting brought from long winter hiding. Green leaves glistened on the bushes and yellow sunlight dappled his path, while the full red begonia blossoms inside the palace railings were like valentines dropped from the hand of a child. Lester stared up at the small white drifts of clouds in the sky, then down at the shimmering blue surface of the pond dotted with children's sailboats, and felt a gathering in his solar plexus like the onset of stage fright.

Pausing to explore this odd sensation he could find, however, nothing out of order. Around him, all was as usual for the season and for the place: a spindly-legged French child went racing by after her hoop, two old men sat in silence over a checker board with half-emptied milk bottles at their sides, and four school-age boys hovered intent as thieves around a marble game in the dust. Yet when two shapely French girls threw back summer jackets to expose the outlines of comely pointed breasts, Lester stirred as though daisies had sprouted from the hard earth at his feet.

This morning had begun as all the others that year, with Francie chirping contentedly over her dolls and Ellen sitting uncomfortably upright in bed with her tray of *petit déjeuner*. Crumbling bits of *croissant,* she had made her usual comment on the bitterness of French coffee, adding that all she could seem to think of these days was her electric percolator at home in Schenectady, and she had then asked if their return tickets for Thursday were in a secure place. He had opened his wallet for her to see, and she had then informed him, as she had so often in the months just past, that there was still money, saved from his research grant, for when they returned home. "No other American here can say *that,*" she'd added, which unaccountably irritated him even though God knows it was true.

She'd continued to drone on in French, which they had long ago agreed to speak together while in France, relating how someone had remarked yesterday that Francie's accent seemed more French than American, and he had considered in silent disloyalty that no one could say this of Ellen's, whose accent was still dreadful. "So this year can be considered a *succès d'estime et de finance,*" she'd gone on to say, handing the pronouncement down as though only she could be the judge of that. Yet now, pausing in the Jardin du Luxembourg, it occurred to Lester that this year had been little different from any other in his academic life. Somehow he had expected to take away more, in terms of life itself, than he had brought with him.

He had lingered too long in the park and now found he would be tardy for lunch—an error one seldom committed at the Pension du Coeur. So, without his usual vigilance for the crazy French drivers, he started across the rue Vaugirard and the next instant was struck by a small French car. Someone screamed, he was carried along for a dizzying moment on the bumper, then rather painfully he was jolted onto the pavement in a most undignified sprawl.

Almost at once, an embarrassing number of passers-by assembled—it was astonishing how many Parisians could gather around in so brief a time—but luckily, no one from the pension was there and, luckily too, he supposed he was all right. He'd had the wind jolted out of him and for a moment there was a slight clouding of his vision which he traced to the fact that his glasses had been knocked off. Someone handed these to him, unbroken, and as he was helped to his feet he was so grateful that he thanked everyone, including the frightened and certainly guilty driver before he hurried on to the pension where he would now be ten minutes late.

Simone was removing the first course when he appeared in the dining room and she narrowed her blue eyes with cold reproach as he apologized. Ellen looked disapproving, but Mlle du Coeur greeted him with a shrug, as though life were not necessarily a ledger in which a man must account for every moment of his day. He was uncommonly relieved about this, and without mentioning the incident, turned from Ellen to Francie, now holding up her plump arms to greet him.

"Papa! Papa!" she cried. *"Ici! À côté de moi!"* She was a loving little girl who nearly always did what was expected of her, yet at this moment her words stirred in Lester a feeling of annoyance. In Schenectady ten days from now, her French speech and mannerisms would seem affectedly out of place, but with Ellen looking on he could not say this. Quickly he sat down and poured wine into his glass, surprised to find that his hand was trembling.

At the far end of the table some of his colleagues were discussing a play they'd seen together the night before; as usual, he and Ellen had not been included. Earlier, they had been part of those evenings at theaters and operas and concerts, had been asked for *apéritifs* before dinner in the rooms of fellow Americans, but once Ellen began making excuses not to go, they were no longer invited. And suddenly the injustice of this burst over Lester like a rocket. Hadn't they all worked like moles through the long dark winter days, sweated equally in the heat of summer through tunnels of documents at the Sorbonne, the Bibliothèque Nationale and the museums? Hadn't he, as well as they, earned what release they could get, what respite for tired nerves and strained eyes and brains in a year that had been all work and almost no play? Yet when the others had gone out to relax and have fun in this Paris that had drawn them like the sun, Ellen had scoffed at such weaknesses and saved their money for the return home!

"You missed the radishes," she was informing him, her pale lips parted birdlike at the centers. "What made you late today, Lester?" she asked, and he stared at her with rising dislike.

"Some stuff I'd overlooked. Not much time left," he said, tight-jawed, turning from the sight of her anxious, no longer pretty face.

"Papa, aujourd'hui j'ai vu trois oiseaux," Francie announced, and it was then Lester pushed away from the table.

"Birds, Francie, *birds!*" he said almost harshly. "You'd better start speaking English now, today, or you'll have one hell of a time when you get back home!"

Francie was startled only for an instant, then said obediently, "Birds, Papa," with a forgiving smile. Only Ellen's hand froze in the act of raising her watered wine to her lips, and then she put down her glass. Francie went on happily chattering to Mademoiselle in French, but Lester, to avoid seeing Ellen's shocked and offended face, looked beyond her to the far end of the table. There two new arrivals were seated, one an American woman he'd seen before, a familiar pension type, dry-skinned and sharply alert; the other a girl of the sort who did not ordinarily appear in a French establishment of the quality of Mme and Mlle du Coeur's. The French were the greatest snobs in the world, he reflected, and got their reputation for tolerance simply because they did not really see anyone below the salt. Yet here was a girl with long untidy hair in a black turtleneck sweater which emphasized quite astonishing breasts, and the look she gave him even from that distance was bolder than usually cast among respectable people. Hastily he looked down, yet when he whispered to Francie in an apologetic voice, "Were the birds pink or green, little one?" he found his tension had lessened.

"*Bleus, Papa! Verts, tu dis!*" Francie whispered back, giggling, and leaned against him with her curls soft against his cheek. Over her head he saw that the strange girl's eyes were still upon him.

Mlle Jacqueline du Coeur permitted herself a brief stir of affection for the serious Professor Clarke, which was most rare in her attitude toward the Americans. Like a nurse who sees her patients only for those brief periods when they are not on familiar ground, she understood that she would be forgotten when they returned home; thus it was not safe to be touched at heart by either child or man. Yet this slender, quiet-voiced professor with his shining big forehead, his smooth dark hair and face long as a Frenchman's of the Academy, disarmed her as others had not. Seeming more

weary than most from his year's work, his blue eyes behind
the glasses too often rimmed with fatigue, he seemed to
enjoy none of the small pleasures to which a man is entitled
—yet today he was certainly savoring the roast gigot!
Mademoiselle watched as he placed the succulent pink
brown bit in his mouth, looked reflective, then pleased; and
soon there was not a morsel left on his plate! If it were not
so strongly a tradition of the pension that one portion only
could be served, Mademoiselle would have ordered Simone
to return with the platter!

As the Professor then expelled a small but contented sigh,
she looked quickly at Mrs. Clarke to see if she, also, had
noticed the important thing. But *non*, the American wife
kept her eyes lowered on her plate as one who shows bravery
under fire, and Mademoiselle wanted to shake her. She
neither liked nor disliked American women—some had become *les bonnes amies* over the passing years—but Mrs.
Clarke was a fool. A French wife of any age would respond
when her man came in with unexpected appetite and the
sap of summer rising in his eyes—and something else, which
merited attention today, as though some part of him had
newly come alive. (Spinster that she was, she knew such
things happened in some men's beginning middle age.)

"I'll go up now, Lester," Mrs. Clarke was saying, sounding her injured note. "Francie, come soon," she added, almost plaintively, in English.

"*Oui, Maman.*"

"Oh, Ellen," called little Mrs. Cook from her side of the
table. "Why don't you go with us to that perfume shop on
the rue de la Paix this afternoon? You may never get back
to Paris, you know—and we're going to the Galeries Lafayette, later, where they're having sales, same as at home."

For an instant Mlle du Coeur waited in hope as Mrs.
Clarke seemed almost to consider. But then she shook her

head, a slight frown between her brows. "I'd love to, Amanda. But I've still got such a lot to do."

"I'd say you have things pretty well in hand, Ellen," Lester said, seeing the look which passed between Mademoiselle and Amanda Cook. It wouldn't hurt Ellen to do what other women did for a change.

"We're setting out about three-thirty if you change your mind," said Amanda, but Ellen seemed not to hear as she hurried from the room.

Lester started to follow, then decided recklessly to stay and have coffee at the table. He did, after all, have a headache, whether from the sun or maybe from the shaking-up he'd got he did not know, but at the moment he needed something stronger than Ellen's Nescafé ritualistically brewed over the spirit lamp in their bedroom.

"Mrs. Clarke tires easily," said Mademoiselle, after most of the others too, had left the table. "For such a young woman, that is too bad," she said, with the false sympathy of a Frenchwoman.

"Well, I shouldn't have snapped at Francie like that," Lester admitted, feeling sudden guilt. "But it's true, you know. If she rattles off nothing but French when she gets home the kids will give her a bad time." Mademoiselle nodded with complete understanding and for a moment Lester relaxed. They were alone at the table now, except for the girl in the black sweater at the far end who was having coffee too; but then she spoke, shattering the mood.

"I'd sure be proud of a kid like that," she said, and got up, bringing her coffee cup with her. "Mind if I join you?" she asked. "I'm Lili." Perhaps she was only trying to be friendly, but Mademoiselle's eyes became cold as an army major's when a private has overstepped his rank. When the young woman took the chair Ellen had abandoned, no further talk was possible. Lester hurriedly finished his coffee and left, excusing himself without looking at the girl, but somehow he was not surprised to hear the Frenchwoman speak to her in a tone of reprimand as he hurried from the room.

In the high-ceilinged, plush-curtained, fifth floor bedroom, Ellen was lying on the Empire bed with her arms rigidly at her sides. "Did you enjoy the coffee?" she asked. "Is it still three francs, or has that gone up like everything else in this miserable place?"

"Still three francs. But I saved the sugar," Lester joked, handing two lumps to Francie, who tossed them happily into her pink mouth.

Ellen flounced over in a movement which sent the thin dark nylon skirt up over her muscle-drawn legs. "It's not my fault we don't have a lot of things," she accused him. Then her voice began to rise. "*You're* the one who fussed about how careful we'd have to be when we left home. You're the one who worried about the money, said we'd have to save!"

"How much have we saved?" he asked, but he did not care. It was only long ago at the beginning, when this year in Paris had been a barely possible dream, that he had felt concerned. Now, thinking how many processes of the brain were required to change dollars into francs, to compute last week's expenses and plan ahead to next, he wanted to say that it was not for this that he'd dreamed of France.

"Eleven hundred and twenty-five dollars!" announced Ellen, raising her voice in triumph. Then she added, accusingly, "That is, if you don't tip foolishly going home, as you did coming over!"

At the exact moment a vagrant breeze passed over Lester's face he began to swear, his hands clenched in the pockets of his brown tweed, five-year-old American suit.

"Christ," he said, quietly at first. Then louder, "Goddam!
Goddam! Shit!"

"Francie, run to your room," commanded Ellen, but Lester had already turned to the door.

"Don't bother, Francie, *I'm* going!" he shouted, heady
with his own rage. If there had been time, he might even
have paused in astonishment to reflect on it.

"Go then," cried Ellen, her little pale mouth drawn thin,
the lipstick not repaired since lunch. "And take your
money!" She picked up her purse and flung it toward him.
"Spend it, throw it all away! I'm the one who's been lonely
and bored; I'm the one who's hated this dirty, cheating
France. What fun have I had here away from home, a whole
year out of my life?"

For a brief moment Lester paused to consider: what fun
had she had when you stopped to think of it? What fun
was she capable of having, he thought, recklessly drawing a
bunch of bills from the handbag she'd thrown at him; but
he did not look at her. If he did he might still regret his
words and his actions, come to terms as he always had, believing that whatever she did or had not done was for their
common good. Yet now, knowing her unlovely and unlov-
ing, the strange brew that had been working in his brain
since morning burst its bounds, ejecting him from the room
like a cork released from a champagne bottle.

In that first moment of escape, Lester took a deep breath;
but in the second, finding himself standing outside on the
Paris street with no destination and no plan, he felt silly.
This seeming freedom was no more real than the impossible
illusion which had brought them to Paris in the first place,
and when a cloud briefly obscured the sun he had half a
mind to turn back. The fact of the matter was that he had
no place to go, and the longer he put off returning the

angrier and more unapproachable Ellen would become. But
then he saw the girl in the black sweater start toward him
and he fled, walking briskly in the opposite direction toward
the bus stop. She reached him anyway, while they were still
in sight of the pension.

"Pardon me," she said, holding out a piece of English
hotel stationery. "I wonder if *you* can tell me where this
place is?" She looked even more exotic out in the daylight,
but younger too, tossing her hair back over her shoulders as
she watched him with close and slightly frowning attention.
He had to take the paper and read the address. "Probably
in the Montmartre district," he said, and handed the paper
back, hoping no one from the pension came along. "Afraid
I can't be of much help there."

"Well, I'm just killing time anyway today," she said, and
started walking along beside him. "I don't like to settle
down to anything so fast—not on my first day back."

"Back?" He was somehow trapped into asking this.

"Oh, I've been over in London for a year. Those English
girls don't give you half a break though," she said, as if he
would know what she was talking about.

"Don't they? Well—that's too bad"; and Lester ran to
catch the bus which providentially had just stopped at the
corner.

Some of the pleasure came back to his senses as he wandered about Paris that afternoon, even though the bright-
ness of the day made his headache worse. As he passed the
little tables anchored under café awnings away from the
sun, seeing idle men and women sitting with hands curled
about their *fines* and *café filtres* and *citrons pressés*, he was
tempted to stop also, but did not. He always felt silly at a
small table alone—but it seemed his headache might go
away if he could sit quietly awhile in the shade. Instead, he

skirted the fountains and stepped over children's toys strew-
ing the paths of the Tuileries with the sun flooding one side
and dark shadows massed on the other and felt an unaccountable nostalgia for this France he had never really
known. Even when he went into the Jeu de Paume to see
his favorite Impressionists, he was not appeased; and by five
o'clock, in a depression, he started back to the pension.

Yet even then he took the wrong bus which carried him
to the far side of the Luxembourg and, tired as he was, this
depressed him almost unendurably. He would have to walk
all the way across the park again, and he was not sure he
had that much energy left.

Passing other miniature tables spread out beneath café
awnings, he saw again the girl in the black sweater sitting
moodily against the old yellow plastered back wall of a very
dingy café. She saw him, but made no move; if she had, if
she'd made any gesture to attract his attention he would
probably have hurried on as before, but sunk in her own
thoughts she represented no threat but simply an excuse to
rest a moment from a sudden vertigo which attacked him.
So with only slight diffidence Lester walked back to the
girl's table and asked, "Mind if I join you for a beer?"

"Have a chair," she said with a shrug, and turned again
to brooding over the busy street.

"Did you find what you were looking for?" he asked,
after a moment of uncomfortable silence. He felt somewhat
better, sitting down.

"No," she said, and then turned her odd smile directly on
him. "Did you, Professor?" But what had he been looking
for?

"Oh, I just went to a picture gallery," he said. "And
walked a bit—Then I took the wrong bus home." Home;
could a pension be called home? And would this girl expect
to walk back with him now, so it would seem they'd spent

the afternoon together, after all? "Did you think *I* was looking for something?" he asked, sitting up stiffly in his chair.

"Isn't everybody?" she asked, without much point; but then she went on to say almost accusingly, "Did you know that old Frenchwoman said she didn't have any rooms vacant in your pension?"

"Why, no," said Lester in surprise. He recalled one had been vacated just the day before on the sixth floor, and wondered how this could have slipped Mademoiselle's mind; at least the girl would not be returning with him. "She must have rented the vacant one before you came—"

"Anyway, it was dull," said the girl. "I want some place a lot livelier than that." She stretched and ran her hand back under the long black hair, lifting it sensuously from her neck. "I know what's here, if you take the time to find it. It won't take me long—"

I'll bet it won't, one part of his mind responded with a side glance at the girl, who really did not look quite respectable; but the other part was puzzling over what she'd said. Dull? Was the pension dull? True, in Mlle du Coeur's neat reception room where the floor was polished daily with lemon-scented oil, in the high-ceilinged bedrooms with their massive bourgeois beds and at the table where old-world formality was imposed on young and old alike, nothing very exciting ever happened. But he had not thought it dull (only he himself was that).

He leaned forward with earnestness to confess this to the girl, and suddenly she grinned. Out on the street cacaphonous noises of traffic and laughter and cursing, a car's backfiring and racing of motors, a policeman's imperative whistle and a burst of profanity close by, hit his nerves and set up a tingling in his spine; but, he thought, at least it's not dull here, and I'm still in Paris. A crazy wave of laugh-

ter swept over him then as though the bump on his head a
few hours back had opened up depths of amusement he had
not known he possessed. The girl had the good sense to
laugh too, and even when he saw they were attracting attention Lester could not stifle the laughter that engulfed
him until he'd paid the check and they were on their feet
weaving out between the tables; then the waiter tapped him
on the shoulder. *"Bonne chance, Monsieur!"* he offered with
a big, exaggerated wink, and this set them off again as they
walked in the opposite direction from the Pension du Coeur.

They had been walking for a long time, it seemed, when
Lester paused to wonder where they were. The girl had been
relating with astonishing familiarity what she thought of
English and American men, and now she was asking what
he thought of French girls and of Paris. He had to admit he
didn't know much of either and this did not sound funny,
but rather sad. "I spend most of my time in museums," he
admitted, trying to speak lightly.

"Museums!" she mocked him, and took his arm in a
friendly way. "Maybe you'd like to go back to your museums now?"

"No," he said looking at her, thinking she really was a
remarkably natural kind of person—but not particularly
pretty. Lester liked pretty women, when he thought about
them at all; still he felt safer with those who were not, and
had often fled from his prettier students. He did not think
he would have to flee from Lili, even though she did have
such a frivolous name, which he had just remembered.
"Lili suits you, you know," he said, dishonestly perhaps.

"That's why I took it," said the girl, to his surprise. The
people he knew did not "take" names but kept those that
were given them at birth and he paused to examine her
candor. "Remarkable," he said, and added, "My name is

Lester." Briefly he wondered if this were a name he'd have "taken" if he could have made a choice. He was not sure that he would.

"Righto, Les," said the girl—an abbreviation he did not usually care for either.

A bus stopped at the corner and they ran to catch it, jumping on the back platform where the lurching start threw them almost into each other's arms. For a moment the girl stood close against him and did not move; surely it was intentional, and once they were inside Lester felt a certain guilt that he had reacted to her, even if briefly. Stiffly he took from his pocket the bus map he always carried, and pointed out to the girl that they were going in the wrong direction; they must get off at once or he would miss the evening meal. He could not afford to be late again, today, he explained carefully, but he was charmed by how adaptable the girl was. She jumped down ahead of him so cheerfully at the next stop that he felt he had misjudged her, so quickly he suggested a beer at a nearby café, being cautious enough to add, however, "Time for one only, I'm afraid." She pranced ahead of him into the dark recesses of the bistro; but then to his surprise she ordered, for both of them, Pernods, not beer. "Well, cheers," she said when the milky stuff was put before them.

"Cheers," he responded, uneasily, seeing now it would take more time than he had thought to get away—but he had not ever really cared for beer.

"I'll tell you something," he said, leaning forward. "When I came out this afternoon I was pretty upset—you know, the way one can feel sometimes, irrational, emotional, resentful somehow. Oh, quite without cause," he added hastily so that she wouldn't think he was implying any fault in Ellen. "But the odd thing—the really disturbing thing was that I actually could not think of anything

I wanted to do! Here I was in Paris on a fine day, a beautiful city—and I couldn't think of one single place to go,
or one single thing I *wanted* to do. I was sick and tired of
all the places I'd seen—in Paris!—sick of the kind of thing
I'd done all my life." He paused, then said recklessly, "Sick
even of the kind of person I seem to have become!"

"That's about how I sized it up," said the girl, nodding. "I could tell you were upset—and you sure did look
fed up."

"You saw that?" he asked, in amazement. "Lili, I felt like
a man who's put all his money on a train ticket, but doesn't
ever quite catch that train. He always gets there too late, as
one train after another leaves the station crowded with
other people who've got no better right to seats than he
has!"

He spoke so heatedly now that at first he did not see the
motorcycle roaring down the quiet street until from the
other direction a gray Citroën came speeding too as though
a blind driver was at the wheel. The cycle reared like a horse
and the cyclist barely recovered to avoid a collision and
certain death as the car screeched burning brakes to a stop.
Why, he might have been killed, thought Lester, his attention diverted, and then with astonishment thought—I too
might have been killed this morning!

This morning: and as the cyclist picked himself up hurling curses at the car and its driver before he roared off to
some other, perhaps more fatal encounter, Lester thought:
But why did *I* have to feel responsible for my driver's
wrongs? "Why should I feel responsibility for everything
that happens in this world?" he asked the girl with sudden
indignation, and she nodded as though she understood that
too. She even put her hand over his, and he put his other
hand on hers, but then something began happening to his
vision, set the rooftops opposite dancing in a strange top-

heavy way, and he felt an awful vertigo; and the next instant everything around him seemed fading out of sight.

"Say, are you all right?" asked Lili, leaning forward, her face no more than a strange blur before his eyes.

With an effort Lester straightened his back and took a deep but uncertain breath; blessedly the evening air was cooler now, half reviving him, and he managed to assert, valiantly, "Never felt better." In a moment this was true. The waiter removed their empty glasses and set fresh drinks before them, which he did not recall ordering, but he drank the licorice tasting stuff quickly, thinking that perhaps this was the only drink that could at the moment restore him. Then, perhaps because he'd wondered in passing if Pernod was expensive, he thought of Ellen again, and somewhat unsteadily rose to his feet. "Excuse me," he said. "I've got to make a call."

Simone answered at the pension, complaining that he was late, but that the ladies had gone out for the afternoon and had not returned either, and her outrage at this—it was easier for a Frenchwoman to blame a woman than a man— so absorbed her that he dared to announce simply that he would not be there for dinner at all.

"Then I will remove your plate," said the Breton as though it could not possibly matter, but he could imagine her thin annoyed lips drawn to the vanishing point.

Lili sat as he had left her and for a moment he paused and observed the girl unseen, the upward slant to her heavy lidded eyes, the sculptured lips so curiously immobile, and wondered what thoughts she might be having there in silence. Even when he sat again beside her she remained a mood, not quite a person, brooding out over the street filling with Parisians coming from their evening meals. It almost seemed a spell was upon her, and he felt a strangeness in himself which seemed compounded of many things—of what had happened to him this morning, of Paris and of old regrets; even if he were not quite certain what it was that he regretted. That he had not cursed the reckless driver of the car but had apologized instead? That he had not earlier known a girl as sympathetic as Lili for other nights this Paris year; or that he must so soon leave this year behind? That he was no different than he had ever been, and perhaps now might never be? All this, perhaps and more: then suddenly he knew. He felt like a boy when a fishing trip has ended and there has not been time enough to fish the finest pool still lying just beyond the bend. . . .

"Sure you're all right?" asked the girl, and Lester said yes, he believed that he was; and then she brought her face close to his in an unexpectedly disturbing way. "Then tell me," she demanded, "have you ever seen anything like Paris at night, Lester? And if not—would you like for me to show it to you—before you die?" He knew why her eyes disturbed him then when, by accident perhaps, her knee pressed slowly against his.

. . . It was no accident, he knew, and now was the time to retreat. Perhaps he had even been waiting for this sort of thing, wondering when, not if, it would happen, and now it had. But he would play it safe, he would not let her know the panic that had started up in him.

"Before I die—in Schenectady," he acknowledged, and clicked his glass against hers so that she would not notice when he drew back his chair and his knee as well. But then she pushed back too and quite gaily got to her feet. So all was well; but he was not quite prepared for his unsteadiness as they stood together, nor the vertigo which again unsettled him and caused him to lurch rather absurdly to one side. Lili put her arm under his shoulder to bring his full weight against her, but he drew away insisting he could stand alone. Rather brusquely he said he needed no help from anyone, not then, not even if the truth were known. "And that means the Foundation people too," he heard himself say as though she would know what the hell he was talking about.

"A man's got to stand on his own two feet," he asserted, but now he knew he'd had too much to drink—three Pernods he'd had; still he was sober enough to see how the stranger across the street was staring at him through American horn-rimmed glasses. Lester felt like shouting that he could mind his own business, except that one knee got out of order and he had to lean on Lili whether he wanted to or not while she called a cab; Lester thought it was a big joke when the taxi swerved around the impertinent stranger and he had to jump back. Then he heard Lili give an address to the driver, the address she'd asked him about a long, long time ago.

The driver turned around slowly and stared. "*Mais*—it will not be there now," he said with a disapproving shake of his head. "Since *le grand Charles,* such places are no more. You will see, you and the drunk." He sounded uncommonly wise or Lester would have taken offense; and when they arrived at last on the street to see a sign on the door that the place had been closed by the police, it was obvious the driver had known what he was talking about.

"*Merde!*" exclaimed Lili as the cab sped away with its smirking driver, and Lester drew the girl against him in sympathy. Even Ellen would have been profane in the face of such disappointment—although she, no doubt would have leveled the blame for it on him. Yet he was not comfortable when Lili recovered so rapidly that he found her body pressing closer to his, and he drew back, giving her a small scolding shake. She was only a kid and instinctive as a young animal—but someone ought to tell her that she was too free about some things, warn her against men she met too casually. But when he noticed an odd smile upon her face, in the end he said nothing, particularly when she began laughing again—at what he could not imagine.

He would have left her then or certainly soon after, if they'd not come on a clean lighted café where the smell of cooking came out like the wagging tail of a friendly dog and the proprietor stood in the door like a man who knows what goes on in his own kitchen. "I'm starved," said Lili, and they went inside and ordered; then Lester went again to the telephone on the wall.

Ellen answered this time, and the odd thing was that she didn't sound angry. She said she'd been expecting him to call for the last half hour, but she spoke as though this were a natural thing.

"Well—I may not be home until late tonight," he said, trying to sound casual, but uncomfortably certain that he did not. "Prepare yourself for a bit of a shock, Ellen. I'm afraid—"

"You're on a binge," she chided him, sounding not a bit like *her*self. If she were another woman he might have wondered if she had a lover! "Those French bars," she went on, "I've seen how men pile into *them*. Well, have a good time —Francie can sleep with me tonight and you can take her bed—when you come in."

A brief vision of the two of them in the fastness of their room made him understand it was madness to keep on any longer with this girl searching for some door which might open—and then close and never let him go; yet he felt he had been let down by Ellen now, committed even by her to go on into this night.

"Take care of yourself," she said, still in that light, false, high tone of voice. "Good night, dear!" And she hung up. So it was with something like self-pity that he returned to Lili.

They had their dinner, and a bottle of wine, and an hour later they stumbled back into the street, night-dark and desperately deserted. Lester was relieved to see the lights of a boulevard ahead, but before he could direct Lili there she'd hailed another cab and given the driver a new address obtained from the proprietor of the café, so there was nothing he could do now except fall asleep in the cab, feeling safe in Lili's hands.

He awoke when the cab stopped in a respectable neighborhood, Neuilly perhaps or some other suburb; but for a moment he could not think what he was doing there. Lili jumped out and stared up at the villa behind the iron fence with a look of cool speculation before she nodded with satisfaction and pushed the bell at the side of a gate. "This is probably it," she said. "It's the way these places look now over in London too." They were admitted by a buzzing and, inside, crossed a graveled path to a formal and elaborately varnished door.

There were murmured voices before the door was opened a crack as though someone from within inspected them, and Lili hurriedly gave a man's name Lester had not heard before. Then they were admitted, squeezing into a small vestibule filled with lights so extraordinarily dazzling it took them a moment to get used to the glare and also to the inspection of two hard-faced men standing before another door. But when that door was opened on a fantastically mirrored room they were startled by seeing pink nude figures reflected in strange movements in the mirrors, as shocking as a Pompeian freize writhing into life. Then that door closed behind them.

For a moment Lester was reassured to see a few other apparently normal men and women sitting, immobilized, it's true, but at least fully clothed, at small tables around the mirrored wall. Then the nude and fleshly creatures were upon them, squealing, hissing, swaying grotesquely and Lester looked fearfully for some refuge. He was glad at last to be seated at one of the tiny red lacquered tables although he had not yet looked at Lili. It could not have been for a place like this that she had been searching, all that day!

For a while they were left alone, and the sport, they understood, was in watching new arrivals as startled as himself in the face of those great flying breasts, thighs scissoring in motion and feet tripping in extravagantly high-heeled shoes. One Negress wore a white satin blouse buttoned primly to the throat which ended where the narrow loin cloths of other girls began and Lester, not knowing where to turn, started in alarm as he heard a shout from a young man in a gray flannel suit seated in a distant corner of the room. Flinging wide his arms he yelled in a deep Southern voice, "Be good to me, baby, good, y'heah?" to the Negress in white satin, and with all eyes fastened upon her she took a gold leather purse from between her thighs and pointed into it. The gray-suited man stuffed in paper francs and she then permitted him to put his arms around her waist, as the other girls squealed in laughter and approval.

"Take him away!" they cried, but the Negress instead slipped out of the man's hold and left him, her shoulders shaking with laughter as she replaced the purse. A moment later she sat beside a scholarly looking Englishman who, with a remarkable air of bored detachment, began to fondle her breasts through the shiny, white satin blouse.

Lester was afraid to look at Lili now, afraid to look anywhere, but when she said, almost reflectively: "She gets well paid for that, you know. That's quite an act she puts on," he turned in astonishment. She had spoken with almost a professional appreciation and her expression in the mirrors opposite, among the red and gold frescoed dragons, was

detached as a woman's who is looking through a shop window. Then she leaned against him with a sudden, almost
mischievous smile.

"You are seeing Paris now, you know, Professor," she
said, her voice low and oddly maternal. "There aren't many
of these places left—this could be the last. Are you having
fun?" He ventured a look into her eyes but could see nothing there to show what she was feeling, either of pleasure or
dismay.

"Yes," he said bravely, having just recalled a Modern
Language meeting where someone had mentioned a place
like this some years ago. Then another teacher had spoken
up and said such places could not exist under de Gaulle.
"Born twenty years too late," someone had complained
facetiously, and the others had laughed. . . . But now as the
small mosaics of mirrors distorted the incredibly licentious
movements of the women Lester knew what this place was,
and knew also that he had to leave. There was no safe way
that he could look, neither at the women, nor at the mirrors
where other faces were blank and not friendly at all, nor at
Lili, but he had seen enough. "What do you say we push on
now?" he asked, but somehow knowing it would be useless
to ask. "I've really got to get back," he said, and it was true.
It was midnight or later—also his head felt very light and
strange and he wanted to go to bed.

But now as at a signal the women, like a covey of squealing birds, converged upon them. Even the Negress left the
scholarly looking man who stared back into his glass with
the pallor of death upon his face, and then they were all
around Lester chattering in several languages and Lili was
saying with almost a wifely smile: "They want the rich
American to order champagne for them. And after that—"
She leaned against him and he felt her warmth and, almost,
some frightening response within himself. "They'll take us

downstairs and you'll see, Les, they'll show you then the things there are to see!"

Downstairs? Into Lester's muddled mind flashed some mythology of man forever lost to dear ones by descent into the underworld and all his Presbyterian ancestors rose in outrage. Yet he could not move, hemmed in as he was with Lili's hand upon his knee and two women leaning heavily on his back, their bare, scented arms about his neck and their breasts pressing even as he struggled to get free. . . .

"Better look to your wallet, lad," he heard, and spun around to see the unconcerned expression of a young man who must have spoken out of a corner of his mouth, since he was looking remote as though he'd not said a word. But there on the seat between them was Lester's billfold, the wallet that held his and Ellen's money and their tickets home. No one else was looking at it, although some one must have put it there, he knew, as Lili moved her hand beneath the table on his thigh.

Clutching his billfold in perspiring hands Lester almost violently moved back his chair but still he could not get quite free and the women squealed with delight. The waiter was pulling a cork from the champagne which set them off again, pressing around him with glasses held out and shriek-ing to pour the champagne from the bottle which the waiter inexplicably had thrust into his hand. Lester poured it all, spilling much of it in his haste, but then there was another bottle opened which he got rid of too while the Negress whispered with Lili, and then each had a hand on him. Lester managed to stand even though they tried to push him down again toward Lili's mocking smile until with a mighty effort he was on his feet with the waiters demand-ing every franc he had.

They wanted even more money when he reached the door

but when he showed them there was nothing left they let
him go; and a moment later the door was opened and he
was thrust out into the star-studded August night where
he stood on the gravel path weak and trembling. But someone followed and stood beside him in the dark and he felt
a strong firm hand upon his arm—a man's hand.

"Take it easy, Mac," the stranger said in a good English
voice. "Thought you needed a bit of help in there. You
were a marked man, old boy. You know that, don't you?"

Lester wanted to thank him but then he became ill in the
path. When he straightened up the stranger led him out
through the gate and then signaled a cruising cab in the
distance.

"The girl stayed behind," he said, although Lester had
not asked. "She'll be with her own kind, I'd say. I guess that
doesn't surprise you!"

"No," said Lester. "Thanks very much," and he made an
attempt to stand more solidly on his feet.

"Any money left? I mean, did you carry any outside of
that wallet?"

Lester shook his head and in panic showed the stranger
that the wallet was empty except for the tickets which were
still there. "I wonder—" Before he could ask, the stranger
handed him several bills. "Tell me your name," said Lester,
gratefully. "I'll return this money early tomorrow morning."

The stranger for the first time laughed. "My name?
When we met in a place like that? Hardly—And I don't
want to know yours either, chum. Better forget the whole
thing. You're well out of it, you know. Go home and sleep
it off. You'll be all right in the morning."

A cab stopped, and by the time Lester was inside the
stranger had disappeared back through the dark silent gate,

which was the last thing Lester remembered clearly for the rest of the night.

He awoke next morning in Francie's room with his clothes neatly folded on the chair beside his bed and some vague memory of Ellen's competent hands, without anger, helping him to undress. On another chair he found a cup of cold coffee and a croissant which must have been left hours before. Now it was after eleven, and there were no sounds of life in the adjoining room.

Sitting up in bed, he ate the roll, then tested his feet on the floor as one trying to stand after an operation. His legs, miraculously, were firm, his head, after he drank the cold coffee, seemed only slightly muddled, and the headache which had pursued him all the day before was gone.

He walked to the window and looked out upon the court where a young woman was hanging red and blue children's socks across an iron bar outside her window, her bare arms reflecting the golden quality of the sunny day. Simone, her dark hair skinned back from her thin face, was sweeping the court vigorously mumbling grievances, as usual. It was a fine day, for so late in the summer.

Lester turned and stared in the large oval mirror to see what of the night before might be revealed in his face. There was more color than usual in his cheeks and chin, but no sign of Bacchus upon his brow, no sensual guilt in his eyes, although a slight uneasiness did appear when he stared at himself too long. As he turned away, he saw their luggage, packed, stacked neatly in a corner and he thought how in another three days they would be at sea. Another ten days and he would be in his office on the college campus looking out on the rose garden and briefly he wondered if the roses had done well the year he'd been away.

The breeze stirred the tired white curtains of this room

in the pension, already somehow misty, like something remembered from the past. The present; was it here? Outside, the leaves of a young chestnut tree in the courtyard danced, and he thought also of the great elms outside his windows in Schenectady. What was the French word for elm?—But what difference did it make since he'd known it all his life in English? All winter long he had been apologizing for not knowing the words for things in French—and for not being rich enough, for not knowing his way around the arrondissements, for not *being* French. But the breeze across his college campus would be cooler than the one barely stirring the curtains here, more fragrant; maybe, after all, he was ready to go home.

It was not quite that simple, though, he knew, as he sat in a corner café and drank hot breakfast coffee. He still had Ellen to face: Ellen, who was difficult, but who lived only for him and Francie. Even if she were angry—and she had a right to be—he must be patient, repentant, and make it up to her some way. She was too good a wife for an academic man, he conceded, to lose now; and he shuddered, quite physically, to think what he had escaped. Another hour with that girl and perhaps he might never have come home again!

He was in perfect control of himself as he entered the dining salon on time for his lunch an hour later. His colleagues and their families were seating themselves with their usual pleasantries, but somehow they looked more drab than usual today, and he no longer envied them. Indeed he felt curiously content; but as time wore on and Ellen and Francie did not appear, he fought back an increasing state of nervousness.

But at last Francie came rushing in dressed in her best dress, and asked quaintly, in English, "Papa, *how are you?* Mama and I saw you while you were sleeping. . . . You looked so funny in my bed." She could not have been coached to say this so that everyone might hear!

"Where is Mama?" he asked, hastily. "Isn't she coming? Is she all right?" he asked, in sudden concern.

"She is coming," said the child, then popped her hand over her mouth, squeezing her eyes shut with laughter. "You wait, Papa," she cried. "Just you wait. It's a surprise!"

He saw Amanda Cook put one finger to her lips and Mlle du Coeur twinkle; but still Ellen did not come.

"What became of that young woman who arrived yesterday when I did?" asked Miss Smith from the far end of the table. "Has she gone already?"

Primly Mlle Jacqueline pursed her lips, casting a rather disconcerting look at Lester. "That young woman will not return here. Sometimes they come in like that from the street, you know—thinking to find something which is no part of the Pension du Coeur. We are forced to speak at once, of course, to say we are sorry, but we do not, after all, have the rooms for this type."

Miss Smith gasped in fascination. "You mean she was soliciting—for money, Mam'selle?" she cried with delight, and the other faces around the table became equally alert and alarmed.

Mademoiselle nodded primly. "It was my belief that this was so. And certainly Mama would not wish for such a person to remain here in her home."

I don't believe it, Lester silently protested. Why, Lili wasn't that bad. She wasn't after money—at least not from me, he thought. Then a curious feeling of pride came to his mind. Even if she were what Mademoiselle implied, the girl had had the whole of the pension to choose from, hadn't she? And she'd chosen him! Slyly he looked around the table at his colleagues whom he'd been foolish enough to envy the day before: what did *they* know of Paris with their cautious little excursions, their carefully budgeted "indulgences" to concerts and cafés, always with the same crowd, safe enough, together? What places had they seen that any tourist could not see who followed the usual dull, conventional path? What had any of them risked in the dark secret hours of a night with a girl like Lili?

"Ah, Madame," Mademoiselle exclaimed, looking up behind him. *"Comme vous êtes jolie comme ça! Regardez, Meester Clarke. Regardez votre femme!"* the French-woman insisted as Ellen slid into her chair and then Lester indeed stared, seeing her pretty again in a soft pink dress, her hair more golden than in her youth and her face flushed with excitement—or was it makeup? Francie jumped up and down, no longer a well-mannered French child, but a little American girl who will not be restrained.

"Jolie maman, jolie maman!" Francie chanted, and then Ellen met his eyes with a frightened, apologetic look which astonished him. "Lester," she said in a low voice, when the others tactfully looked away. "I've something awful to tell you." Why, her expression was foolish and beseeching as a girl's and for a moment Lester stared with interest—but warily, too.

"What is it, Ellen?" he asked, quite gently, wondering how long this rather disarming humility might remain.

"That money we saved—" Ellen took a deep breath as he nodded, but her voice was very low. "I spent it!"

He examined this surprising statement and then decided it was safe to look at her more closely. "Yes, I see you must have," he agreed, thoughtfully.

"Amanda and I went shopping yesterday. Dior was having their annual sale," she said. "Then—then I went to Antoine's and had myself—done over. And I bought more clothes at the Galeries Lafayette, and perfumes and—I bought you a very nice tie," she said, looking as though she might cry. "Oh, I *don't* know what came over me!" But suddenly remembering: "It wasn't until this morning that the concierge told me you'd been hit by a car yesterday on the rue Vaugirard. And I saw then that was why you were —why you weren't yourself. Oh, you should have told me! Lester, are you all right now?" she asked emotionally.

"I think so," he said, gravely, aware that he must now, and no doubt for some time to come, choose his words to Ellen with care. "It was just a scratch. Although it did shake me up a bit. But you look fine, Ellen. It's what you should have done when we first came."

"Oh, Lester, I'd never forgive myself if you were hurt!"

"Well, I was shaken up, and I don't exactly remember all that happened after that—Until this morning," he said, cautiously taking pleasure in his deceit. "But don't worry about me. Anyway, I'm all right now."

"Oh, Lester—" But luckily she took him at his word. "I did save enough money for the boat train," she whispered then. "I didn't spend *quite* all of it, you know."

"Good. Then we'll still get home all right," he said, nodding, and Francie clapped her hands and Mademoiselle nodded too, no longer pretending she had not been listening —and marveling once again at the tolerance of American husbands. Conversation around the table was noisily resumed, and others began praising Ellen's looks as though they had all been friends here from the start.

"Lester," Ellen whispered after a while. "You can't imagine what those shops are like. Everyone was so friendly, and so helpful, too. These French—I don't think they really dislike Americans, you know. Not the way we thought."

"Only the poor ones," he conceded, smiling, but this vexed her and she went on to something else.

"The important thing," she said, "is that at last I *have*

seen Paris. Oh, Lester, I hated going home and having nothing to tell anyone about this wonderful civilization."

"Maybe we'd better go to the Folies-Bergères tonight,"
he suggested. "If you've got that much money left. And if
you're up to it."

Tenderly she regarded him. "Oh, yes. But what have you
seen?" she asked from the height of her new sophistication.
"I spent the money. I had all the fun. Yes, let's *do* go to the
Folies tonight. Then *you'll* have some Paris memories too!"

She was still Ellen, he saw, taking everything on herself,
her pleasures, or the ones she permitted him, the only ones
to matter. What difference does it make? he asked himself
as he ordered coffee for them both, uncomfortably aware
that her increasing animation was becoming rather too girl-
ish now with repetition.

For how she talked! On and on she told Mademoiselle, in
rapid English which the Frenchwoman had difficulty following, every detail of her shopping expedition, and Lester
listened with increasing uneasiness; even Ellen should realize
after a while how often she was repeating herself.

Still she talked, about the cost of things, about what
people said to her and she to them, all the impulses she must
have been holding back these winter and summer months
spilling out, surprising everyone. Then it occurred to him
that she was only rehearsing what she would tell back home
in Schenectady, embroidering the tale (he could see this by
a few startled glances from Amanda Cook), making her
year in Paris sound glamorous enough to arouse the envy of
other faculty wives. And finally, with horrified premoni-
tion, Lester understood that he would have to hear this story
endlessly in the years to come, and that the future would
be a never diminishing account of Ellen's last days in Paris.

It was in that moment of despair that Lester felt a pang
of regret that what he himself had experienced must forever

be kept locked within his mind. How would it have been last night, he wondered, if he had not run away but had let Lili and the women lead him down those stairs? What things would he have seen, what things would he have done? What might he then have had to take away from Paris?

Lili had chosen him, he thought again. Lili. And perhaps it was only natural that a wave of tenderness swept over him as though she were his only love.